Teknon and the Champion Warriors

Mentor Guide

8 SESSIONS TO LAUNCH YOUR SON INTO COURAGEOUS MANHOOD

A companion leader's guide for *Teknon and the CHAMPION Warriors*

A **Mission Guide** for sons is also available

Teknon and the CHAMPION Warriors Mentor Guide — Father

© 2000, 2006, 2015 Brent Sapp. All rights reserved.

No part of this book may be reproduced, stored in a retrieval system, or transmitted in any form or by any means electronic, mechanical, photocopying, recording, or otherwise, without prior permission from the publisher.

Published by Generations of Virtue
www.generationsofvirtue.org

Author: Brent Sapp
Editors: Megan Briggs and the Generations of Virtue team
Illustrator: Sergio Cariello
Designer: Generations of Virtue

ISBN 9780984896059
(previously ISBN 9780976614371)

Printed in the United States of America.

Most of the content of the Just Do It! appendix is taken from Would You Like to Know God Personally?, a version of the Four Spiritual Laws, written by Bill Bright. Copyright © 1965, 1968, Campus Crusade for Christ, Inc. All rights reserved.

Most Scripture quotations are taken from the New American Standard Bible.

© 1960, 1962, 1963, 1968, 1971, 1972, 1973, 1975, 1977, 1994 by The Lockman Foundation. All rights reserved. Used by permission.

The following Bible versions are also used:

NIV — Scripture quotations marked (NIV) are taken from The Holy Bible, New International Version®. NIV®. Copyright © 1973, 1978, 1984 by International Bible Society. Used by permission of Zondervan Publishing House. All rights reserved.

TLB — Verses marked (TLB) are taken from The Living Bible © 1971. Used by permission of Tyndale House Publishers, Inc., Wheaton, IL 60189. All rights reserved.

www.generationsofvirtue.org

*The CHAMPION Training
adventure program
is dedicated to a pair of champions —
my mom and dad*

Teknon and the Champion Warriors

Mentor Guide—Father
8 sessions to launch your son into courageous manhood

Table of Contents

Aiming Your Arrow foreword
by Dennis Rainey

Mentor Preparation

Planning Your Son's CHAMPION Training

Chapter One M8
    The 60 Day CHAMPION Training Program
        Timetable M9

Chapter Two M10
    I'm Waiting for You, Dad
        My Wake-up Call M10
        My Son's Response to
        the CHAMPION Adventure M12

Chapter Three M13
How to Approach the CHAMPION Adventure

    Adapting to Unique Situations..............................M14
    Other Male Relatives or Mentors M14
    Mothers M15

Chapter Four M16
How to Use the CHAMPION Training Program

    Pre-training and Preparation.................................M16
    The Night of Challenge M18
    CHAMPION Sessions..M20
    Celebration Ceremony...M22
    Ongoing Involvement M24

Chapter Five.. M26
Father's Arsenal

    CHAMPION Training Commitment....................M27
    Fiction Glossary M28
    Greek Terms in the Story......................................M37
    Guiding Insights Request Letter M39
    Summary of Success..M40

Mission Guide

This section follows the Mentor Preparation section, giving you a page-by-page copy of your son's Mission Guide. You will be working from the same material as your son except that we have given you the answers to the questions as well as notes and tips in the margins.

Sessions 1-8 .... 1 through 127

Foreword

Aiming Your Arrow

Congratulations! You hold in your hands a powerful, life-changing tool—a way to impact your son for a lifetime and leave a mighty legacy for future generations.

The psalmist tells us that our children are like "arrows in the hands of a warrior" (Psalm 127:4). Our culture is in dire need of young men who know who they are and where they're going. What better way to launch your son into young adulthood than with a planned adventure resource like this one? It's a great way to direct your son toward godly character and convictions.

You're in for a few months of dynamic interaction with your son. It may be hard at times and you might feel you're in over your head, but you'll find all the resources you need in your Mentor Guide. Your son will probably tire from time to time, and you may, too. But stay with it! You can't help but draw closer to God and closer to each other through the course of this study.

Men, the time is now. You can do it! With the proper preparation and a planned trajectory, you can watch your "arrow" take flight.

Dennis Rainey
Executive Director, FamilyLife

Teknon and the Champion Warriors

Mentor Preparation

Planning Your Son's Champion Training

Chapter One

The 60 Day CHAMPION Training Program

This CHAMPION Training Program helps to prepare your son for young adulthood. It's a 60 day, interactive adventure designed to equip your son to understand the basics of godly character and convictions for his life, under your guidance. The CHAMPION Training 2 month program also develops a "communication habit" between father and son about the most important topics in life.

The eight CHAMPION qualities, built around an acrostic of the word "CHAMPION," are defined in the CHAMPION Code (see page 6 in the *Mission Guide* section). For the purpose of this program, "character" is defined as moral strength that grows out of our relationship with God. Personal growth is expressed through the physical, emotional, social, mental, and especially spiritual areas of our lives.

The CHAMPION Training also provides an opportunity to formally celebrate your son's transition into young manhood with a ceremony assembled to honor him. Robert Lewis, in his excellent book *Raising a Modern Day Knight*, writes about a young manhood ceremony: "Ceremony should be one of the crown jewels for helping a boy become a man. In many cultures throughout history, a teenage boy is taken through some type of ritual to mark his official passage into manhood. I believe one of the great tragedies of the western culture today is the absence of this type of ceremony."

It is our privilege and responsibility as fathers to prepare our sons for young adulthood and to celebrate their transition into this important stage of life. You will interact regularly with your son over the next two months on issues that are important to him. From my own experience with my two sons, as well as other dads' experiences with their sons around the world, I can affirm this process will help to open lines of meaningful communication, deepen your relationship, and launch a life-long friendship.

The CHAMPION Training program consists of three fully integrated resources:

- ▲ *Teknon and the CHAMPION Warriors* fiction book—15 action-packed episodes
- ▲ *Mission Guide* for your son—8 CHAMPION Sessions linked to the fiction episodes
- ▲ *Mentor Guide* for you—Everything you need to plan and carry out the 60 day program, including the contents of the *Mission Guide* with answers and tips.

Timetable

There are several approaches that you can take with your son's CHAMPION Training. The CHAMPION program is designed as a two-month exercise based on weekly meetings with you and your son. A 60 day program provides a specified objective with a clear timeframe. Both father and son are more likely to maintain focus, and less likely to become distracted. You can also meet bi-weekly or monthly if you prefer; but I highly suggest the 60 day time frame.

> *Example is not the main thing in influencing others. It is the only thing.*
> Albert Schweitzer

Chapter Two

I'm Waiting for You, Dad

My Wake-up Call

My call came in 1995, when I paused from the normal frantic pace of life to experience one of those, "When did this happen?" revelations. I glanced across our living room to see a mature-looking 11-year-old boy. He was 5′ 6″ tall, with feet almost as big as mine. His voice sounded a little lower than I remembered. It seemed like yesterday when he rode a miniature fire truck around the driveway, yelling at me to watch him. Now he was reading novels, taking more showers, and excelling in basketball. My son, Casey, was becoming a young man.

I didn't see it coming. *Wait a minute*, I thought to myself, *I'm not ready for this*! In two years my son Casey would be a teenager. What had I done to prepare him for such a major transition? Did he have the knowledge and skills to enter young manhood? Had he heard me verbalize my priorities and values? Was he ready to face the inevitable temptations that society, the online universe, and his peers would offer him?

I've long admired the Jewish tradition of the bar mitzvah. As a Jewish boy approaches his teenage years, he engages in a program of rigorous academic training based on Jewish tradition and beliefs. At the end of his training, the boy recites some difficult Hebrew passages and then reads a speech he's prepared describing why he's ready to become a young man. Then, a ceremony takes place. At the ceremony the boy's father formally acknowledges to his friends and family that his son is a young man. In essence, the father communicates to everyone present that the boy is ready to assume the privileges and responsibilities that come with his new stage in life. It's a powerful moment!

The more I thought about the richness of tradition involved with the bar mitzvah, the more I wanted Casey to experience a transition like that. I wanted him to enter young adulthood with a sense of direction and purpose. The description of Jesus in his early years provided the ultimate example for my son: "And Jesus grew in wisdom and stature, and in favor with God and men." (Luke 2:52).

According to this passage of Scripture, Jesus set the pattern for us to follow as He grew in wisdom (mentally), in stature (physically), in favor with God (spiritually), and in favor with man (socially/emotionally). As Casey entered his early teen years I wanted him to establish a foundation of skills and principles to use in the years ahead—socially, mentally, physically, emotionally, and most importantly, spiritually. Finally, I wanted Casey to experience a formal celebration of his young adulthood. Not that he would become a man at 12 or 13, but that he would recognize that he was no longer a child and that he must start learning, and practicing, what it means to be a godly man.

I decided to write down all of the elements I felt Casey needed to make his training complete. I detailed character qualities to develop, activities to accomplish, books to read, and movies to watch. I also wrote down the names of men, individuals I knew and trusted, whom I wanted to play a role in Casey's development.

You are probably experiencing the same type of wake-up call that I experienced a few years ago. You may feel, as I did, that you need a practical manual to help you think through the issues of guiding your son as he transitions into young manhood. Today boys must make tough decisions at a progressively younger age. They must decide early what they will and will not watch, listen to, and believe.

It is my hope that the *Teknon and the CHAMPION Warriors* adventure will help you in this process. I commend you for caring enough about your son to take the proactive step to complete this training experience with him.

My Son's Response to the CHAMPION Adventure

Here is what my son, Casey, said at age 13 about our CHAMPION adventure together:

> When I started the CHAMPION Training, I was really looking forward to doing it with my dad because I knew it would be a way for us to spend time together. Although we had a very strong relationship before, we were even closer after the training was finished. It was a great experience for me to learn what being a "real man" meant. During the week, we would share and discuss articles from our local newspaper, or a news magazine just to discuss our feelings on different topics. Sometimes we would watch a movie like "Ben Hur" or "Sergeant York" or listen to a talk by Dennis Rainey or Chuck Colson. Every time I watched or listened to what Dad suggested, I got a lot out of it. I learned a lot about my dad and myself during that time.
>
> After the training was finished, I looked back on the previous year and thought about what I had learned from discussing those articles and watching those movies with my dad. It was unbelievable to look back and realize that I had changed spiritually and mentally. If I had to go back and do it all over again, I would not change one thing.

No man will ever rise above the opinion his children have of him.

Dennis Rainey

Chapter Three

How to Approach the CHAMPION Adventure

This is the recommended strategy for your son's 60 Day CHAMPION Training Program.

1. **Pre-training and Preparation (instructions in chapter 4)**
   - ▲ Pray regularly for preparation.
   - ▲ Identify goals and expectations for the experience.
   - ▲ Read the fiction book and review all the program elements and tips in your *Mentor Guide*.
   - ▲ Have a kick-off dinner with your son.
   - ▲ Give your son the fiction book to read (set a target date 2 weeks before your first session).
   - ▲ Set a date for your first CHAMPION Session and ask your son to re-read episode 1 and to complete the session 1 questions in his *Mission Guide* before your session together.

2. **CHAMPION Sessions (instructions in chapter 4)**
   - ▲ Pray before each session.
   - ▲ Prepare before each session by reviewing that session in this *Mentor Guide*.
   - ▲ Have your son prepare before each session using his *Mission Guide*.

3. **Celebration Ceremony (instructions in chapter 4)**
   - ▲ Prepare for your son's celebration.
   - ▲ Schedule your son's celebration after he has completed all the sessions with you.

Adapting to Unique Situations

While this program is designed to be used by a father and son in a one-on-one mentoring situation, it can be adapted and used effectively in other settings.

Other Male Relatives or Mentors

There will be boys who do not have a father that can take them through the CHAMPION Training. This is a significant ministry opportunity for an uncle, grandfather, or other male relative to step in and mentor this boy. In addition, godly men who are friends of the family could also take the challenge of mentoring a young man in this situation. You will need to explain to the young man that the *Mission Guide* uses the words "son" and "father" often, but that you are adapting this material so that you can participate with him and invest in his life.

A special word for adoptive fathers or stepfathers: I understand there are additional challenges for you as an adoptive father or stepfather to use the CHAMPION Training. Even if you do not refer to each other as father and son, remind the young man that God has a special plan for your family and has blessed your life and your home with him. Communicate how much you care about him and that you are using this CHAMPION Training to help him to be all God intended for him to be. God Himself set the model for adoption (or step-fathering). It's one of His greatest gifts (see Galatians 4:5-7).

Mothers

Mothers truly deserve respect and encouragement in the task of raising a son. If you are a mother who wishes to provide the CHAMPION Training to her son but lacks adequate adult male participation, I applaud your desire to invest in your son's life.

There are three basic alternatives available as a mother to expose your son to this training:

- ▲ Approach a spiritually mature adult man in your community, or a trusted relative, to lead your son through the program. Pray that God would provide someone to whom your son connects and whom he respects. (See the Other Male Relatives or Mentors section above.)

- ▲ Facilitate the training program yourself. If you choose this option, it might be best if you approach it somewhat like a homeschool teacher. A lot will depend upon the level of openness that you have with your son on male issues. Concentrate on the content; present the material to your son as an academic project that you and he can discuss together. Understand ahead of time, however, that the story line is decidedly male-oriented, with a science fiction flavor. Work to deepen your relationship with your son, but try to enlist male mentors to engage and augment your efforts as needed. Explain to your son that the *Mission Guide* uses the word "father" often, but that you are adapting this material so that you can participate with him and invest in his life.

- ▲ Approach your pastor or a spiritually mature adult man in your church who is willing to invest in the lives of several young men. With some extra planning and creativity, these boys could be trained in a group setting.

Remember, above all, that God is capable of providing for your needs in this area. He will honor your love for your son and your obedience to Him!

How to Use the CHAMPION Training Program

The following instructions are provided to help you to succeed in every facet of the CHAMPION Training program with your son.

Pre-training and Preparation

Pray regularly for a month in preparation

Prayer is the first and most important step in your preparation. It will also be essential throughout the course of the CHAMPION Training. Psalm 127:1a tells us, "Unless the Lord builds the house, they labor in vain who build it."

Identify the targets for your son's adventure

Ask yourself one question: "What's the primary thing I want to accomplish in my son's CHAMPION Training?"

If you understand what you want to accomplish with your son through the CHAMPION Training ahead of time, your target will become more clear and your efforts more directed.

> *Build me a son, O Lord, who will be strong enough to know when he is weak, and brave enough to face himself when he is afraid, one who will be proud and unbending in honest defeat, and humble and gentle in victory.*
>
> General Douglas MacArthur

Read the fiction book and review your Mentor Guide

Read through the story *Teknon and the CHAMPION Warriors*. Then carefully review the *Mentor Guide*.

Brent and Casey's Story

Before Casey started his training I realized that sharing great books, tapes, and movies with him meant nothing if he yawned at the challenge. So I "pre-sold" him on the idea. I kindled his interest on several occasions by saying, "Casey, next month I'm going to challenge you to an adventure that you and I will take on together. If you accept the challenge, it will be hard work, but it will also be a lot of fun. None of your friends have experienced anything like this. If you complete the adventure with me, you will be ready for young manhood. We will also celebrate your completion of the task." That's all I said. Over the next few weeks, Casey wanted more information, but I kept telling him, "You'll receive your challenge soon." By the time we set a date to formalize the proposition, Casey was primed for the task.

The Night of Challenge

Create a Night of Challenge to kick off your son's CHAMPION Training. Think carefully through the challenge you will present to your son. This challenge will create the "tone" of importance for your son's training, and encourage him that he's important enough for you to invest this time with him. Here are some tips for this important evening:

- ▲ Tell your son that he has a unique opportunity to undertake a training adventure with you that will prepare him to be a successful young man.
- ▲ Give him the *Teknon and the CHAMPION Warriors* fiction book and ask him to read through it.
- ▲ Show him the *Mission Guide* and explain the format (highlight the direct tie to the fiction book, the interactive discussion questions, and the fun "maneuvers").
- ▲ Discuss with him how often you would meet and the length of time it would take to complete the CHAMPION Training (two months).
- ▲ Remind him that this will be a project between the two of you.
- ▲ Make it clear that completing his training will require work, but it will be a lot of fun and worth the effort.
- ▲ Explain that if he completes the training you will honor his accomplishment with a special celebration in his honor.

If your son declines the challenge, ask him why, but don't press him. He may not understand his need yet or he may feel he isn't ready. Bide your time, continue to pray for him, and revisit your proposal at a later date. If your son accepts the challenge, both of you should sign the CHAMPION Training Commitment form (in chapter 5). This agreement will provide your son with a visible reference to the commitment he is making.

Schedule your first CHAMPION Session together and ask your son to read or re-read the first episode of *Teknon and the CHAMPION Warriors* if he hasn't already. Give him his *Mission Guide* and ask him to complete the questions as best he can in session 1 before your first CHAMPION Session.

Explain to him that both of you are making a commitment. Describe how Green Berets, fighter pilots, and Olympic athletes labor diligently to attain the distinction of their rank. Describe to him that no worthy prize is gained without significant effort.

NOTE: The primary premise of selling anything to anybody is that only an unmet need will motivate him to act. We must create a desire in our sons by motivating them and helping them to identify their need for the CHAMPION Training. Communicate your interest in this adventure to your son by:

- ▲ **Enthusiasm** — Your excitement about your son engaging in the CHAMPION Training will become contagious.

- ▲ **Encouragement** — Reinforce your belief in him and your belief that he can complete his training.

- ▲ **Example** — As your son sees your desire to live the life of a CHAMPION yourself, he will also want to become a CHAMPION.

Brent and Casey's Story

We went to one of our favorite restaurants and chose a table in the corner. I pulled out the materials and walked him through the concept of CHAMPION Training. To my surprise (and relief) he was thrilled with the idea. I knew Casey wouldn't completely understand what was ahead in his training. But what he did understand excited him, and that excited me.

I promised Casey that if he finished the training I would put together a celebration that would honor his accomplishment. I also committed to give him a CHAMPION Symbol, a pendant or ring, representing his accomplishment and recognizing his becoming a young man.

CHAMPION Sessions

CHAMPION Sessions are the heart of the CHAMPION Training.

Meet regularly: If possible, meet with your son every other week for your CHAMPION Sessions once you start. Plan for at least one hour and no more than two.

Make it your own: Customize and make this training your own. Holidays, vacations, and occasional business trips can make it difficult to maintain a rigid schedule for our meetings. Your son may grow weary. If so, take a break! This training is about character development and relationship building, not completing a project. Be flexible and creative with the location and setting.

Remember that the suggestions offered in this book concerning how to conduct your son's training are just that—suggestions. You can customize your son's training to meet his particular needs and temperament. If you have an idea for an outside activity or a tool to use in your son's training, by all means use it.

Elements of a CHAMPION Session

- ▲ **CHAMPION Characteristics and The CHAMPION Warrior Creed**—Several character traits are highlighted for each session.

- ▲ **Story Summary**—The fiction episode is summarized only in your *Mentor Guide*, not in your son's *Mission Guide*.

- ▲ **Discussion Topics**—Key subjects are summarized in both guides, with additional context provided only in your *Mentor Guide*. Each question in the *Mentor Guide* includes a possible answer. These are only suggestions. Facilitate the discussion with your son as you see fit.

- ▲ **Reconnaissance**—Reconnaissance (or "recon") is a military activity in which a soldier explores an area to gather important information for the mission ahead. In this section you and your son will discuss this week's episode from Teknon and the CHAMPION Warriors.

- ▲ **Strategy and Tactics**—Strategy refers to the overall planning of a mission. "Tactics" refers to the methods used to secure the objectives planned out in the strategy. In this section you and your son will discuss specific CHAMPION characteristics, investigate strategies and tactics from the Bible, and discover how to apply them in your son's life.

▲ CHAMPION Training Commitment Form — A sample agreement between you and your son to complete the CHAMPION Training

▲ Fiction Glossary — A list of words, pronunciations, and definitions for characters and terms used in the story

▲ Greek Terms in the Story — A summary of the character and location names derived from Greek terms and their meanings

▲ Guiding Insights Request Letter — A sample letter for soliciting special participation from people for your son's celebration ceremony

▲ Summary of Success — A sample presentation for your son's celebration ceremony that summarizes key points of accomplishment through the CHAMPION Training.

Brent and Casey's Story

Sometimes we took our CHAMPION Sessions on the road. One memorable night, we went to a diner after an Orlando Magic basketball game. We pulled out our Mission Guide at 11:00 p.m. in a booth at the back of the restaurant. The waitress noticed that Casey had polished off his milkshake in short order. In an unprecedented gesture, she offered to let Casey drink as many shakes as he could for the price of one. What a night! Basketball, milkshakes, CHAMPION Training, and lots of laughs.

Casey and I had potholes to navigate on the road to the final celebration. Holidays, vacations, and occasional business trips made it difficult to maintain a rigid schedule for our meetings. And, as is the case with most lengthy projects, there came a time when Casey grew weary and resistant to completing his task. At one point, we decided to take a break for a few weeks. However, because of the value he saw in the training, the fun we were having, and his previous commitment to finish, he pressed on and completed his CHAMPION Training. I was very proud of him! We began to plan for his celebration ceremony.

Celebration Ceremony

At the end of your CHAMPION Training, take time to plan an appropriate celebration ceremony for your son. This event is essential to your son's transition to young adulthood; it will be one of those key markers in his life that he will never forget. Author and speaker Robert Lewis says, "A man is not a man until his father says that he is." This is your opportunity to announce to your son, and to those who attend his ceremony, that he has now made the transition into young manhood and that you are proud of him.

Suggestions for your son's celebration ceremony:

- ▲ **Setting** — Where will the ceremony take place? Will you have food, and if so, what will it be? What atmosphere do you want to create for the ceremony?
- ▲ **Script** — Determine the format of the ceremony. What events will you include and in what order?
- ▲ **Speakers** — Will someone speak? What will they say? In what manner will they say it — in person, on video, on audio recording, in writing? (Refer to the Guiding Insights Letter in chapter 5.)
- ▲ **Summary of Success** — Take time to write a short speech documenting some of the highlights of your son's training. (Refer to the Summary of Success sample in chapter 5.)
- ▲ **Symbol** — Will his CHAMPION Symbol be a ring, pendant, plaque, custom coin or some other gift? One father created a custom CHAMPION Coin to give to his son.
- ▲ **Special Finale** — What fun, memorable activity will you do together to top off the celebration? What would your son really enjoy? (Don't just choose something that you would enjoy doing with him.)

Brainstorm with your son about his celebration about halfway through his training. Let him have input into the format to heighten his enthusiasm, but make sure you leave enough room for the element of surprise. If you plan to give him a CHAMPION Symbol at the celebration, let your son know that you plan to have it and what it will be. This CHAMPION Symbol can become a significant motivator for your son to complete the program.

Brent and Casey's Story

Even though it took extensive preparation, Casey's celebration was an event we will never forget. First, I sent a request ahead of time to close friends and relatives around the country. Casey either knew these men, or had heard me talk about them. I asked them to film themselves and answer these three questions for Casey:

1. *If you were Casey's age again, what would you do differently?*
2. *What skills would you recommend that Casey develop?*
3. *What is the single most important thing for Casey to remember as a young adult?*

Casey heard from the men that had the greatest impact on his father's life. The next step was to find a location for the celebration. One of my friends told me about a wilderness ranch owned by another friend. We were able to secure the ranch for the date I set.

On the night of the celebration, I kept Casey in the dark about the details. I picked him up at 7:00 p.m. from a youth meeting and took him out to the ranch. On the way out, I played the videos containing insights and encouragement from my friends. Casey enjoyed their talks immensely. First, a friend of 20 years spoke. Next came Casey's uncle. As we entered the ranch, we turned off the videos and got out to greet the men I had invited to join us. We feasted on Casey's favorite foods: barbecue, brownies, and IBC root beer.

After dinner I played another video, and this time Casey heard from the man who led me to Christ more than two decades before. Then, each man at the ranch in turn took Casey on a short walk to share his specific insights and encouragement. One of the men gave him a compass to remind him to keep his focus on the "True North" of the Word. Another gave him a pocketknife. All gave him the pearls of their experience. As the last walk finished, we gathered around the fire, and I asked Casey to recite the characteristics of a CHAMPION Warrior.

I followed with a short prepared speech, recalling the benefits and highlights of the training we experienced together. I gave Casey his ring, and we all prayed for him. The men hoisted Casey above their shoulders and marched around the fire.

> *We capped off the night with a wild hog hunt on the ranch. Until that night, Casey and I had never had the thrill of chasing a 175-pound animal that smelled like an unwashed tennis shoe and looked like a rototiller with fur. We bagged one, or I should say our hosts bagged one, and let us share in the glory. It was a great night!*

Ongoing Involvement

(Post-Training)

The completion of this stage marks the end of your role as a trainer in your son's life. Certainly there will be other opportunities to teach during his teen years and beyond, but your role transitions from trainer to coach in the later teen and young adult years. In other words, after the early teen years, parents primarily coach and encourage those principles and skills that they have already taught their children.

To a great extent the CHAMPION Training is like a delayed fuse. It is essential to communicate the importance of developing courage, mental toughness, and purity during the early teen years. Depending on his age and circumstances, your son may not have had the opportunity to apply many of these principles in his life yet. He may not even understand the reason for covering some of the CHAMPION topics. Ideally, the training helps your son to develop godly character and set his convictions before he encounters problems. For example, your son may not have been tempted yet to view pornography, but he will understand the danger of doing so after you and he complete session 4. Then later, when one of his peers encourages him to visit a porn site, the delayed fuse of your previous discussion will ignite.

Brent and Casey's Story

My son Casey is now a man; and I'm very proud of the godly man he has become. He's an adventurer down to his bootstraps. He lived three years in China, learning Mandarin and traveling to the far ends of the Eastern empire. I'm also very proud of my son Kyle, who completed his CHAMPION Training with two of his friends and their dads. Kyle is also a godly man now and adventurous like his brother. Kyle is a talented singer and musician. Casey and Kyle are both businessmen seeking to make their impact on the world for God. I am convinced that the investment I have made in Casey and Kyle's life will continue to produce long-term returns, which in the years to come will dwarf any compensation I could ever receive from my career or other pursuits.

Generations of Virtue

Refer to Generations of Virtue (www.generationsofvirtue.org) for the best resources to reinforce your son's CHAMPION Training.

Father's Arsenal

This section includes:

CHAMPION Training Commitment Form

Fiction Glossary

Greek Terms in the Story

Guiding Insights Request Letter (Sample)

Summary of Success (Sample Presentation)

The CHAMPION Symbol

CHAMPION Training Commitment

I, _____ agree to participate in CHAMPION Training.
    (son's name)

I understand what is expected of me, and I accept this responsibility with enthusiasm and expectation. I will attempt at all times to approach challenges and successes with a positive attitude and dependence on God. I recognize that my father's role is to encourage, help, and mentor me.

I commit to complete my assigned tasks and interact with my father during our CHAMPION Sessions. I look forward to what God will teach me in my CHAMPION Training. I am excited about our adventure together and the celebration that awaits me at the end of my training.

I, _____, agree to lead _____,
   (father's name)   (son's name)

in his CHAMPION Training. I understand what is expected of me, and I accept this responsibility with enthusiasm and expectation. I will attempt at all times to approach my son's challenges and successes with a positive attitude and dependence on God. While my son must take responsibility to gain the most from his training, I realize that I need to help him succeed and to be available to support him in any way that I can.

I am committed to prayer, preparation, and personal involvement in guiding the CHAMPION Training. I look forward to regularly interacting with my son and to what God will teach both him and me in the coming year. At the end of my son's training, I will celebrate his transition into young manhood with pride and joy.

_____   _____
     (son's signature)   (father's signature)

Date: _____ Mentor/Witness: _____

He will restore the hearts of the fathers to their children and the hearts of the children to their fathers. Malachi 4:6a

Fiction Glossary

Admiral Ago (ăd′mər-əl ā′go) – Chancellor of the planet Basileia and good friend to the CHAMPION movement.

amacho (ə-mä′chō) – Fierce beast that roams Kairos, often hunting in packs. Large claws, powerful legs, and a poisonous barbed tail allow it to prey on other animals.

Ameleo (ä-mē′lē-o) – Overindulgent father of Pikros and Parakoe, who meets the CHAMPION Warriors on the Ergonaut.

amuno (ə-moō′nō) – Fighting style of the CHAMPION Warriors taught to Kratos and then to Teknon by Tor, Epps, Arti, and Matty. Primarily focused on defense, it resembles several martial arts disciplines.

android (ăn′droid) – Mechanical robotic creature.

Apoplonao (ä-pŏp′lŏn-ā′ō) – Perasmian maiden, nicknamed Lana, whom Teknon meets at a spring-fed pool near Bia. Lana is actually Scandalon disguised as a beautiful young lady.

Artios (är′tē-ōs) – Nicknamed Arti, he is a mentor to Teknon and member of the CHAMPION movement. An amuno master from the Mache Region, Arti created a face band that enables him to shoot a paralyzing ray or a beam that identifies individuals or objects cloaked by a holographic image.

Basileia (băs-ĭ′lē-ə) – Home planet of Kratos, Teknon, the mentors, and Magos.

Basileia Technology Institute (BTI) – Famous university on Basileia that produces many of the engineers and inventors for the planet. This is also the school where Kratos and Phil met.

Bia (bē′ə) – Small, rugged town on the planet Kairos where Kratos and Teknon meet the Harpax gang.

bionic (bī-ŏn′ĭk) – Having physical characteristics enhanced by electrical or mechanical components.

biosynthetic matrix (bī´ō-sĭn-thət´ĭk mā´trĭks) – Technology designed by Magos and Kratos that allows a human to merge his mind and body with computer circuitry. Magos further develops this technology to provide what he believed to be mechanized immortality.

CHAMPION (chăm´pē-ən) – One who exhibits Courage, Honor, Attitude, Mental Toughness, Purity, Integrity, Ownership, and Navigation as he battles evil and changes his world for Pneuma's glory.

cyborg (sī´bôrg) – A being that is partly human and partly machine.

Daimons (dā´mənz) – An evil army of aggressors that threatened to overthrow Basileia in the days of the ancient League of CHAMPION Warriors.

Didasko (dī-dăs´kō) – One of the CHAMPION instructors who can be accessed through the Logos.

digmite (dĭg´mīt) – Small, carnivorous insect, capable of inflicting a painful, fever-inducing bite.

dinar (dĭ-när´) – Basic currency used on the planet Basileia.

domicat (dŏm´ə-kăt) – Tame and calm domestic house pet.

Dolios (dō´lē-ōs) – An extremely powerful kako android created by Magos that guards the Logos. Dolios has the ability to appear in the form of his opponent's greatest fear.

Epios (ĕp´ē-ōs) – Nicknamed Epps, he is a mentor to Teknon and a member of the CHAMPION movement. He comes from the Mache Region and is an amuno master. Epps created special gloves that allow him to heal injuries and illnesses, as well as cause the people he touches to become completely honest and friendly for a brief period of time.

Ergo (ûr´gō) – Resort town on the planet Kairos, where Kratos and Matty battle the amachos.

Ergonaut (ûr´gō-nôt) – Cruise ship that shuttles between Ergo and Sarkinos on the planet Kairos.

Eros (ĕr´ōs) – Host of one of the holographic imaging salons in the Sarkinos Underground.

fibronic (fī-brän´ ĭk) – Consisting of a special technology that enables digital transmissions between androids.

footsoldier (foot´ sōl-jər) – Mindless android created by Magos primarily for the purpose of maintaining security for Sheol and destroying his enemies.

florne (flôrn) – White, sweet-smelling, delicious, and soothing drink.

gleukos (gloo´ kōs) – Intoxicating drink that produces a mind-altering effect similar to alcohol or marijuana.

gorgon (gôr´ gŏn) – Dangerous reptilian creature that ranges from five to 10 meters in length.

hammerhoop (hăm´ ər-hoop´) – A popular Basileian sport where opposing teams of three players each attempt to send a spherical "pulsar" into statically energized nets called chambers, as they avoid being swatted by mechanized arms used to guard the chamber area. The game is played in an anti-gravity environment and requires tremendous physical conditioning.

Harpax (här´ păks) – Attractive but vicious race of people, who use their strength and intelligence to hurt, rather than help, others. Harpax usually travel in para-military gangs.

Hedon Bay (hē´ dən bā) – Body of water on the planet Kairos that lies south of the Northron Peninsula and empties into the sea north of the Thumos Mountain range.

Hilarotes (hĭ-lâr´ ə-tēz´) – Teknon's sister, nicknamed Hilly, and daughter of Kratos and Paideia.

hodgebeast (hŏj´ bēst) – Large, aggressive mammal with long tusks that spike upward from its lower jaw. Its fur is short and coarse, and it emits a strong, unpleasant odor.

holographic image (hŏ-lə-grăf´ ĭk ĭm´ ĭj) – Artificial, three-dimensional (3D) representation of a real-life object or environment produced by sophisticated laser technology.

holographic image salon – Establishment where people go to view and interact with sexually oriented holographic images for entertainment.

Hoplon (hŏp´ lŏn) – The highly technical, multi-dimensional shield created by Kratos and Phileo.

hoverboard (hŭv´ er-bôrd) – Aerodynamic piece of sporting equipment used on Basileia to ride snow-covered slopes or the crest of large waves on the coastline.

Hudor Sea (hoo͞´ dôr sē) – Body of water on the planet Kairos that Teknon, Kratos, Matty, and Tor cross on the Ergonaut.

hydronic engine (hī-drŏn´ ĭk ĕn´ jĭn) – Powerful machine that produces its own energy through an ingenious protonic regenerating process developed by Kratos. Because of its capabilities, only three engines are required to maintain the elevated status of the suspended mansion.

hydrovessel (hī´ drō-vĕs´-əl) – Aquatic transport ship propelled by engines that force water through the hull of the ship and out the back.

infra-illuminator (ĭn´ frə-ĭ-loo͞´ mə-nā-tər) – Infrared light device that allows sub-light vision capabilities without revealing its location to surveillance systems.

interactive non-woven alloy – Man-made fiber constructed by Matty to create his suit. The filament is interactive at a molecular level, performing when desired as a chemical catalyst in the body to produce great speed.

Kairos (kī´ ros) – Planet where Kratos, Teknon, and their team battle Magos and attempt to retrieve the Logos.

kako (kā´ kō) – Type of powerful android created by Magos and programmed to carry out his instructions. Kakos have the ability to process information and make decisions. Several, such as Scandalon and Dolios, have special abilities.

keline (kē´ līn) – Domesticated animal on Kairos, which provides delicious meat for consumption.

kilometer (kĭl´ ə-mē´ tər) – Unit of measurement to determine longer distances on Basileia, equal to one thousand meters or 0.62 miles.

Kopto (kŏp´ tō) – Commercial town where Kratos, Teknon, and the rest of their team first arrive on Kairos.

Kopto Commercial Market – Large, outdoor shopping market located in the city of Kopto.

Kratos (krā´tōs) – Father of Teknon and leader of the new CHAMPION movement.

Lacerlazer (lā´ sər-lā´ zər) – Powerful tool used by the Phaskos to penetrate the hard surface of Kairos for the purpose of mining.

Lady Trophos (trō´ fōs) – Owner of the tavern in the Thumos Mountains and an undercover operative working against Magos.

leviathan (lə-vī´ə-thən) – Large, aggressive sea creature that hunts off the Northron coast and is a threat to swimmers.

locator beacon – Small transmitting device that allows Paideia to track Kratos and his team via satellite, wherever they might be.

Logos (lö´ gös) – Small, spherical object that holds all of the teachings of the CHAMPION Warriors.

Maches (mä´ shāz) – Warriors from the Mache Region of Basileia, known as the only remaining tribe on the planet that practices amuno, the fighting style of the ancient CHAMPION Warriors.

Mache Region (mä´ shā rē´ jən) – An isolated and rugged area of Basileia that is home to Tor, Epps, Arti, and Matty.

Magos (mä´ gōs) – Old friend of Kratos, turned evil cyborg (part human, part android) and enemy to the CHAMPION movement. The fixture on the side of Magos' head enables him to control all of the creatures and computer equipment in his empire.

mamonas (mä-mō´ näs) – Valuable mineral used to produce memory chips for highly advanced computer equipment.

Mataios (mä-tā´ ōs) – Nicknamed Matty, he is a mentor to Teknon. Matty comes from the Mache Region and is a member of the CHAMPION movement. Matty created a suit that enables him to attain incredible speed, protective eyewear that gives him 360-degree vision, and boots that allow him to easily scale walls and other vertical surfaces.

mentor (měn′ tôr) – One who helps, teaches, and cares for another person. Teknon's mentors are all committed to helping and training him to become a CHAMPION Warrior.

meter (mē′ tər) – Fundamental unit of measurement to determine length; equivalent to 3.28 feet.

molecular matrix (mə-lĕk′ yə-lər mā′ trĭks) – Cell level structure of a person or object that can be restructured and transmitted via particle assimilator to other locations.

Mount Purgos (mount pûr′ gōs) – Magnificent mountain on the planet of Basileia, near the home of Kratos, Padeia, Teknon, and Hilly.

nela (nē′ lə) – Soothing beverage that can be served either hot or cold, made from the ground leaves of the nela plant grown on Basileia.

neurosynaptic (no͞o′ rō-sĭ-năp′ tĭk) – Pertaining to the process that occurs when transmissions are sent from the brain across the nervous system of the human body and into the devices developed by the various CHAMPION Warriors. For example, the Hoplon responds to Kratos' brain waves.

Northros (nôrth′ rös) – Small, primitive town located on the Northron Peninsula of Kairos, and a temporary stopping place for the CHAMPION Warriors before they entered the Thumos Mountains.

Paideia (pā-dē′ ə) – Wife of Kratos, mother to Teknon, and a member of the CHAMPION team.

Parakoe and Pikros (pâr′ ə-kō) (pĭk′ rōs) – Immature teenage brothers and sons of Ameleo who meet Teknon on the Ergonaut.

Paranomia (pâr-ə-nō′ mē-ə) – Nicknamed Pary, she is the beautiful girl from Northros whom Teknon finds attractive and spends time with.

particle assimilator – Common device designed to transport individuals and objects instantly from one place to another through transformation of their molecular matrix.

Perasmos (pâr-ăs′ mōs) – Thick forest on Kairos that Kratos and Teknon travel through on their way to Bia.

✦ Fiction Glossary ✦

phago (fä´ gō) – Very large reptilian creature with long claws and fangs. It can grow to 25 meters in height and is a natural predator of the amachos.

Phasko (făs´ kō) – Group of mining people located on Kairos. Short and powerful, they have the ability to drill through the ground with incredible speed and accuracy.

Phileo (fĭl-ā´ ō) – Also called Phil, he is a Phasko and long-time friend to Kratos.

Plutos Region (plōō´ tōs rē´ jən) – Tropical territory on the coast of the Hudor Sea where Kratos and Teknon enter the lavish resort of Ergo.

Poroo (pō-rōō´) – Distinguished but arrogant manager of the resort town of Ergo.

Poneros (pə-nâr´ əs) – Inherently sinister, powerful, and brilliant evil master of Magos.

Pneuma (nōō´ mə) – The eternal Warrior King whom the CHAMPION Warriors follow and serve. He is the all-powerful Spirit who desires that all people choose to come into a personal relationship with Him.

Pseudes (sōōds) – Informant for Magos in the Sarkinos Underground who reveals all he knows to the CHAMPION team after Epps touches him with his special gloves.

Rhaima (rā´ mə) – Small planet inhabited by prison colonies.

Rhegma (rĕg´ mə) – Leader of the Harpax gang whom Kratos and Teknon encounter in the town of Bia.

sabercamel (sā´ bər-kăm´ əl) – Tri-hump, foul-smelling, shaggy beast used primarily for transporting cargo across desert terrain.

sandsnipe (sănd´ snīp) – Small, foul-smelling Basileian rodent, which can produce a noxious liquid spray from its nose if provoked.

Sarkinos Underground (sär´ kə-nōs ŭn´ dər-ground´) – Also know as Lower Sarkinos, a popular adult entertainment community on Kairos that offers gambling, luxurious lodging, holographic imaging salons and other forms of illicit entertainment.

Scandalon (skăn′ dl-ŏn) – Kako android and one of Magos' most dangerous creations. Scandalon has the ability to change his appearance to whatever form will cause the most harm to Kratos, Teknon, or whomever else he targets as an enemy. He works primarily through the methods of deception and seduction.

scratchbacks (scrăch′ băks) – Thieves and murderers who form nomadic gangs that roam the dark alleys in urban areas on the planet Basileia.

seismos (sīz′ mōs) – Large, thick-skinned carnivore that roams the Thumos Mountains.

Sensatron (sĕn′ sĭ-trŏn) – Small diagnostic device that Arti carries on his belt. The Sensatron can take many different kinds of readings, including weather, enemy advancement, and material composition.

sheepalopes (shēp′ ə-lōps) – Mindless domestic animals that are used for food and clothing.

Sheol (shē′ ōl) – Fortress and headquarters of Magos located deep in the Thumos Mountains. Sheol can be readily recognized by its three large, sinister towers.

Shocktech (shŏk′ tĕk) – Hand-held weapon purchased by Teknon at the Kopto Commercial Market.

speca (spĕ′ kə) – Basic unit of currency used in the Kopto Commercial Market on the planet of Kairos

spike rat (spīk′ răt) – Small, barely edible rodent found along the trails of Kairos.

swampcrusher (swŏmp′ krŭsh-r) – Carnivorous, multi-tentacled creature that lurks in the rivers of the Basileian rain forests.

tantronic energy (tăn-trŏn′ ĭk ĕn′ ər-jē) – Highly volatile and dangerous power source that can vaporize human flesh if the energy intensity is high enough.

Tarasso (tär-ăs′ ō) – Region on planet Kairos west of the Hudor Sea where the city of Sarkinos is located.

Teknon (tĕk′ nŏn) – Son of Kratos and Paideia and primary character in the story.

ten high – Card game usually associated with gambling and played frequently in the Sarkinos Underground casinos.

Tharreo (thär-rā′ ō) – Nicknamed Tor, this mentor to Teknon is from the Mache Region. He is second in command on the CHAMPION Warrior team and an amuno master. Tor created arm braces that enable him to fire energy beams that can lift and hold tremendous weight. The beams increase Tor's already enormous strength.

Thumos Mountains (tho͞o′ mōs) – Treacherous mountain range on Kairos known for violent weather changes and dangerous terrain.

transfer station – Place where travelers can start and end trips using a particle assimilator.

transtron racer (trăns′ trŏn) – Sleek, fast vehicle that can hover several meters above the ground.

transparent carbonic alloy – Clear, impenetrable man-made substance constructed in a patented process that uses several rare elements found on both Basileia and Kairos.

vealplant (vēl′ plănt) – Delicious vegetable that is large enough to be cut into servings that resemble steaks.

wartmouse (wôrt′ mous) – Small, sharp-toothed rodent capable of eating five times its body weight each day.

Greek Terms in the Story

Following is a translation of Greek terms used in the story *Teknon and the Champion Warriors*. The names for each of the characters and many of the places were selected because of the meaning of those names in the Greek language that was used in the original writing of the New Testament books of the Bible.

- amacho — brawler
- Ameleo — neglectful, careless
- amuno — defend
- Apoplanao — seducer
- Artios — perfect, complete
- Basileia — kingdom
- Bia — violence
- Didasko — teacher
- Dolios — demon
- Epios — gentle, patient
- Harpax — extortioner
- Hilarotes — cheerfulness
- Hoplon — armor, weapons of warfare
- Hudor — water
- Gleukos — wine
- Kairos — God-given opportunity
- kakos — evil, wicked
- Kopto — wail
- Kratos — power, strength (leader)
- Logos — the word (used as a name for God's verbal and written Word)
- Magos — sorcerer
- Mataios — vanity
- Northros — slothful, lazy
- Paideia — instruction
- Parakoe — disobedience
- Paranomia — transgression, iniquity

- Perasmos (spelled pierasmos) — temptation
- phago — gluttonous
- Phasko — affirm
- Phileo — love
- Pikros — bitter
- Pneuma — spirit
- Poneros — evil, malicious
- Poroo — harden
- Pseudes — false, liar
- Rhegma — ruin
- Sarkinos — carnal
- Scandalon (spelled skandalon) — falling, temptation
- seismos — earthquake, tempest
- Sheol (Hebrew word) — world of the dead, grave, pit
- Teknon — child
- Tharreo — boldness, courage, confidence
- Thumos — fierceness, anger
- Trophos — nurse

Guiding Insights Request Letter
(Sample)

Dear _____,

It is with great pride and anticipation that I write this letter to you. My son, _____, will soon celebrate his transition to young manhood. Since (date/month/year) my son has worked through what we call CHAMPION Training. The purpose of _____'s training has been to provide a systematic process to help him transition into young manhood. We have done this by applying biblical principles to help him develop godly character and convictions in his life.

On (month/day) we will have a ceremony to celebrate his accomplishments and to recognize _____ as a young adult. You can be a part of this important event in my son's life.

Would you please take a few minutes to record yourself answering the following three questions?

1. If you were _____'s age again, what would you do differently?
2. What skills would you recommend that _____ develop?
3. What is the most important thing for _____ to remember as a young man?

This video will be played at _____'s celebration ceremony and then packaged as a gift to him. After you finish the recording, please send it back to me by (deadline date and details for delivery. IE: email, file transfer, etc.)

Your participation in _____'s CHAMPION Training would be greatly appreciated by both of us. Thank you in advance.

Sincerely,

Summary of Success
(Sample Presentation)

The Summary of Success is a presentation that you should write and deliver to your son at his CHAMPION Celebration Ceremony. The Summary of Success should encourage your son by recapping the highlights of his CHAMPION Training, while reminding him of important issues you want him to remember. Your son will remember this presentation for years to come.

Following is a portion of what I (Brent) read to my son at his celebration ceremony. This statement now hangs on my son's wall in a frame with a picture of my son and me from his ceremony.

> *Casey, tonight is a special night for both of us. The little bruised bundle that was delivered more than 12 years ago is now standing before me, almost my own height, ready to enter the most adventurous years of his life. We have had a great time together in your training, and we will have many memories ahead.*
>
> *Tonight, you have been encouraged not only by the men here, all of whom I trust and admire, but also by those who have had an impact in my life from all corners of the nation. Don Jacobs, Rex Roffler, Chester Kennedy, Martin Shipman, Roger Berry, Bert Chandler, Nick Repak, Jack McGill, Uncle Bill and finally my own father have all contributed to your celebration. They have given you their pearls, the benefit of their hindsight that can only come from years of experience. Cherish their advice and refer to it often in the years to come.*
>
> *I also encourage you to remember and apply the lessons we learned together over the past three months.*
>
> ▲ *The movies you watched. Keep in mind that the director of a movie is always trying to communicate a message, whether it is encouraging or destructive.*
>
> ▲ *The value of controlling your temper.*
>
> ▲ *The value of thanking people, and how a short note of thanks communicates volumes.*

- *The importance of respecting authority, because God will never make you a leader unless you are a faithful follower.*
- *To constantly challenge yourself. Continue to identify and face the dragons that stand in your path. You have seen time and again that towering dragons reduce to sniveling lizards when they are faced bravely in battle.*
- *In addition to success, there will be times of failure in your life. Three words: recover, recover, and recover.*
- *To continue writing in your journal and keep learning how to express your emotions. Realize that if you can't write it, you don't understand it.*
- *To present yourself always as a faithful steward of the resources God has entrusted to you. Your time, talents, intelligence, and financial possessions should always be used to His glory.*
- *To revere God as part of loving Him.*
- *To keep a high standard of purity, remembering that purity is not only a commandment from God, but also includes tremendous benefits both now and in the future. Keep yourself accountable and honest with me, your mentors, and one or two other Christian friends that you trust.*

There is an old saying that a man is not a man until his father says that he is. As I give you your pendant, representing your training and maturity, I say with love and confidence that you are indeed a young man. Along with these men around you, I am committed to your success and look forward to your progression to full manhood. I love you, Casey.

To paraphrase Psalm 19:13, may God continue to refine your life mission as He keeps you from willful sins as His servant; may they not rule over you.

The CHAMPION Symbol

A fighter pilot shows off the wings pinned on his chest. An Olympic athlete sports his medal. A Green Beret proudly wears a ring on his hand with the Latin phrase De Oppresso Libre (Free the Oppressed) engraved on it. A CHAMPION Symbol is a great way to honor your son's accomplishment in completing the CHAMPION Training. Present it during his celebration ceremony to recognize and commemorate his transition from boyhood into young manhood. This will be a significant and lasting reminder of this milestone in his life, as well as the lessons he has learned with you.

The most meaningful CHAMPION Symbol will be something that your son can wear—a piece of jewelry such as a ring or a pendant. You may locate your own meaningful piece of jewelry or order the specially engraved CHAMPION ring or pendant by going online at www.generationsofvirtue.org.

Teknon and the Champion Warriors

Mission Guide

AN INTERACTIVE ADVENTURE TO EXPLORE COURAGEOUS MANHOOD

A companion study guide for
Teknon and the Champion Warriors

Mission Guide
An Interactive Adventure to Explore Courageous Manhood

TABLE OF CONTENTS

Vital Documents

What is a CHAMPION Warrior? 3

Elements of a CHAMPION Session 4

The CHAMPION Warrior Creed 5

The CHAMPION Code 6

The Map of the Mission 8

The CHAMPION Sheet of Deeds 9

CHAMPION Sessions

Session 1 11

Session 2 25

Session 3 39

Session 4 51

Session 5 69

Session 6 87

Session 7 105

Session 8 119

Appendix A: Just Do It! 128

Appendix B: CHAMPION Training Adventure Program 134

Acknowledgments 135

About the Author and Illustrator 135

What is a Champion Warrior?

What comes to mind when you hear the word *warrior*? Today, that word refers to many things, like the road warrior who just invested his entire savings into an overpriced motorcycle and dominates the road. Or the weekend warrior, an overstuffed couch potato who sits in an overstuffed chair, watching whatever stuff is showing on TV all weekend long. And what comes to mind when you hear the word *champion*? Do you think of the guy who won several gold medals in the Olympics? Or the winner of the Indy 500? Those definitions may be true, but they bear little resemblance to the real warriors and champions of years past.

Many years ago, Native Americans living on the Western plains of the United States rode on horseback into battle when they reached their 14th birthday. A boy trained with his father early in life so that he could assume responsibility, take care of others, and, if necessary, fight to protect the safety of the tribe. These sons were more than teenagers; they were young men, each with the *soul of a warrior*.

In July 1776, General George Washington led his 5,000 troops, many under the age of 15, into battle against 25,000 of the finest soldiers Great Britain had to offer. Washington's outnumbered armed forces courageously held their position and played a vital role in gaining the freedom Americans enjoy today. These brave soldiers were more than teenagers; they were young men, each with the *heart of a champion*.

Since those days, many in our society have lost the vision for developing courageous young men. As a result, young men have not been given the responsibility they are capable of taking on. Many have not been challenged to think big thoughts and dream big dreams. How about you? Are you infected with the venom of low expectations or are you setting high standards for yourself? What are your values? What are your goals? Are you living a life full of challenge, adventure, and fulfillment?

How would you like to become a young man with the soul of a warrior and the heart of a champion? You can! Are you ready to begin the quest toward courageous manhood? Are you willing to invest the time and energy? If so, the CHAMPION Training adventure is for you!

Your *Mission Guide* includes 8 CHAMPION Sessions that you will complete and then discuss with your dad or leader over the course of several weeks.

Elements of a CHAMPION Session

▲ **CHAMPION Characteristics**: One or two key character traits are highlighted for each session.

▲ **Power Verse:** A new Bible verse related to the session for you to memorize.

▲ **Discussion Topics:** Key subjects you will address in the session are summarized.

▲ **Reconnaissance**: Reconnaissance (or "recon") is also a military activity in which a soldier explores an area to gather important information for the mission ahead. In this section you and your dad will discuss an episode from Teknon and the CHAMPION Warriors.

▲ **Strategy and Tactics**: Strategy refers to the overall planning of a mission. Tactics refers to the methods used to secure the objectives planned out in the strategy. In this section you and your dad will discuss specific CHAMPION characteristics, investigate strategies and tactics from the Bible, and discover how to apply them in your life.

▲ **Main Things:** You and your dad will agree on some key principles and an action point you learned from each episode. You can record your action points on the CHAMPION Sheet of Deeds (located on page 9). You can work on applying these action points before your next session, and continue applying them as you develop these deeds for a lifetime as a CHAMPION.

GET READY FOR A CHALLENGING EXPERIENCE THAT WILL CHANGE YOUR LIFE!

The CHAMPION Warrior Creed

"If I have the Courage to face my fears; Honor, which I show to God† and my fellow man; the proper Attitude concerning myself and my circumstances; the Mental Toughness required to make hard decisions; Purity of heart, mind, and body; the Integrity to stand for what I believe, even in the most difficult situations; effective Ownership of all that is entrusted to me; and focused Navigation in order to successfully chart my course in life; I will live as a true CHAMPION Warrior, committed to battling evil, and changing my world for God's glory."

† Note: In the fiction book, Teknon and the CHAMPION Warriors, the Warrior King called Pneuma is a fictional character intended to represent God (Father, Son, and Holy Spirit). For this study, the name Pneuma is only used when referring to the fictional story character.

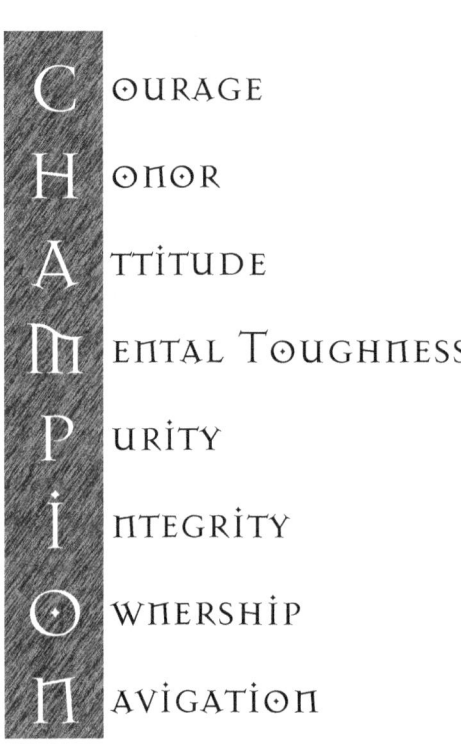

The CHAMPION Code

Character is the moral strength that grows out of our relationship with God.* Personal growth is expressed through the physical, emotional, social, mental, and especially spiritual areas of our lives.

Characteristics of a CHAMPION Warrior

Courage

I will cultivate bravery and trust in God. I will break out of my comfort zone by seeking to conquer my fears. I will learn to recover, recover, and recover again.

Honor

I will honor God by obeying Him and acknowledging Him as the complete source of my life, both now and through eternity. I will treat my parents, siblings, friends, and acquaintances with respect. I will appreciate the strengths and accept the weaknesses of all my "team members."

Attitude

I will cultivate a disposition of humility. I will assume a correct and hopeful view of myself as a member of God's family. I will improve my ability to manage anger and discouragement. I will develop and enjoy an appropriate sense of humor.

Mental Toughness

I will allow God to direct my thinking toward gaining common sense and wisdom. I will use discernment when making hard decisions. I will desire respect from others rather than compromise my convictions for acceptance or approval.

Purity

I will train myself to keep the temple of my body and mind uncorrupted mentally, emotionally, and physically. I commit to avoid and flee sexual temptation.

Integrity

I will seek to acquire a clear understanding of who I am in Christ so that I may have a deeper comprehension of what I believe, what I stand for, and how I can live out those convictions in the most difficult circumstances, whether I am alone or with others. I will allow other people to hold me accountable to standards of excellence.

Ownership

I will apply effective stewardship by using my life and the resources God entrusts to me—including my possessions, time, and talents—for His glory. I will seek contentment in God's provision for my needs. I will learn to practice delayed gratification.

Navigation

I will allow God to chart my course by accepting my mission from Him, and I will complete that mission by trusting in Him. I will study the Bible, God's Word, so I can know Him better and gain His strength and direction for my life. I will become goal-oriented by learning to focus my attention on completing worthwhile short-term and long-term objectives.

*Note: In the fiction book, Teknon and the CHAMPION Warriors, the Warrior King called Pneuma is a fictional character intended to represent God (Father, Son, and Holy Spirit). For this study, the name Pneuma is only used when referring to the fictional story.

The CHAMPION Sheet of Deeds

Following are my personal action points for each session of my CHAMPION Training. I will strive to apply these action points during my training adventure and also will make an effort to continue applying them as I seek to grow in godly character for a lifetime of living as a CHAMPION.

Episode 1: _____

Episode 2: _____

Episode 3: _____

Episode 4: _____

Episode 5: _____

Episode 6: _____

Episode 7: _____

Episode 8: _____

Episode 9: _____

Episode 10: _____

Episode 11: _____

Episode 12: _____

Episode 13: _____

Episode 14: _____

Episode 15: _____

Session 1: Episodes 1 and 2 of Teknon and the CHAMPION Warriors

Episode 1: Destination: Kairos

CHAMPION Characteristics

Courage and Navigation

Power Verse: Philippians 4:6-7

Be anxious for nothing, but in everything by prayer and supplication with thanksgiving let your requests be made known to God. And the peace of God, which surpasses all comprehension, will guard your hearts and your minds in Christ Jesus.

Story Summary

This initial episode introduces most of the primary characters in *Teknon and the CHAMPION Warriors*. As the story begins, we learn that Kratos and his son, Teknon, are journeying to the planet Kairos, accompanied by Teknon's mentors—Tharreo (nicknamed Tor), Epios (Epps), Artios (Arti), and Mataios (Matty). Although we don't know the exact reason for their mission, it appears that the team is preparing to battle an evil threat to their home planet, Basileia. Teknon is somewhat anxious about what awaits them.

Episode 1 Overview:

In this session, you will have the opportunity to discuss with your son the importance of taking responsibility for his actions and attitudes, as well as how to trust God for what is rightly God's responsibility. You'll also be able to explore the process of overcoming fear of the unknown when preparing for a specific challenge.

Do the thing you fear, and fear will die.

Anonymous

Question #2 Tip:

In order for your son to see the value in memorizing the creed, you need to join with him in reading and memorizing it. He will take his cues from you.

Discussion Topics

Prepare for a challenging task

Overcome fear of the unknown

Accept responsibility and trust God with the rest

Optional Exercise

Watch the movie *Iron Will* before with your son before this session. *Iron Will* is an excellent biopic about Will Stoneman, a young man who took responsibility to provide for his family after his father died.

Reconnaissance

1. Review the Map of the Mission on page 8 before beginning this section. Identify where the team is located in episode 1.

2. What is the CHAMPION definition of **Courage**? Of **Navigation**? (Refer to the CHAMPION Code on page 6.)

   Answer for Courage: "I will cultivate bravery and trust in God. I will break out of my comfort zone by seeking to conquer my fears. I will learn to recover, recover, and recover again."

   Answer for Navigation: "I will allow God to chart my course by accepting my mission from Him, and I will complete that mission by trusting in Him. I will study the Bible, God's Word, so I can know Him better and gain His strength and direction for my life. I will become goal-oriented by learning to focus my attention on completing worthwhile short-term and long-term objectives."

3. What is the team's mission on the planet Kairos?

Answer: Judging from Kratos' response to his wife, Paideia, (" ... too much is at stake ... ") the team is pursuing a mission to protect and defend something of great value. They are embarking on a mission that has great risks.

Strategy and Tactics

Take Responsibility

In 1917, Will Stoneman gathered all of his courage as he stepped out of the train and into the frigid Canadian air of Winnipeg, Manitoba. He gazed for a moment at the bright lights and endless activity. At age 17, this rugged farm boy from the hills of South Dakota was about to undertake the greatest challenge of his life. In a few short hours, he would begin a 500-mile dog sled race in hopes of winning the $10,000 first prize.

Will needed the money to save his family's farm and pay for his college education. His father died in a sledding accident only a few weeks earlier, leaving the family without the income from their cabinet-making trade. Now Will was alone in a big city, about to race against the finest sled teams in the world over some of the roughest territory in North America.

QUESTION #3 TIP:

At the end of episode 1, the team is leaving for the planet Kairos. Kairos is a Greek word that refers to a God-given opportunity at a specific point in time. Tell your son about the meaning of Kairos and then discuss question 3.

You may also want to explain that many Greek names appear in this story because the Bible's New Testament was first written in Greek, the key trade and cultural language during the first century A.D.

There lives in each of us a hero, awaiting a call to action.

H. Jackson Brown, Jr.

◆ SESSION 1 ◆

What would most teenagers have said if they were faced with Will's challenge?

What can I do? I'm just a teenager.

It's too late for me to make a difference now.

Even if I tried, I'd probably drop out the first day, so I won't bother.

I don't have the experience. Why can't somebody else race for our family?

Will Stoneman didn't choose to make excuses. He saw an opportunity to help his family, and he jumped at it. He took responsibility to compete in a difficult race, even though he had only a month to prepare for it. During that month, he worked as hard as he could, training himself to race on little food and even less sleep than any of his competitors. He did everything within his ability to contribute to his family's success.

Will's determination shocked the entire country when, against incredible odds, he won the race! His unwillingness to give up, regardless of the circumstances, earned him the nickname "Iron Will."

1. Read James 1:22-26. What happens if we only listen to the Word and do nothing? (See verse 22.)

    Answer: We cannot merely listen to the Word of God; we must take responsibility to obey it. Otherwise, we delude or fool ourselves.

> *Success is peace of mind which is a direct result of self-satisfaction in knowing you made the effort to become the best that you are capable of becoming.*
>
> John Wooden, former Head Coach of UCLA - 10 time National Champions

2. What will happen to the person who takes responsibility to do what the Word says? (See verse 25.)

   Answer: An effectual doer of the Word will be blessed in all he does.

   ┌───┐
   │   │
   │   THE MAIN THING I LEARNED FROM   │
   │   EPISODE 1:   │
   │   │
   │   _____   │
   │   │
   │   _____   │
   │   │
   │   _____   │
   │   │
   │   _____   │
   │   │
   │   _____   │
   │   │
   └───┘

Accept the challenges so that you may feel the exhilaration of victory.

General George S. Patton

MAIN THING:

Help you son by suggesting some key truths that he should have learned during this session, such as what things are his responsibility and what things are God's responsibility, ways to overcome fears and preparation for a challenge.

Episode 2 Overview:

You will have the opportunity during this session to discuss the topic of spiritual warfare with your son. It's vital, as episode 2 brings out, to accurately assess the enemy's capabilities. Satan, our brilliant enemy, is plotting to ruin as many people as he can. We must not underestimate Satan and his desire to cause our demise. We live in a sinful world, and it's important for us to understand Satan's strategies in deception and temptation.

However, you will be able to encourage your son with the knowledge that our all-powerful God has defeated Satan through Christ's death on the cross. Even though we will face daily spiritual battles concerning issues of right and wrong, we can remember that God has already won the war (Romans 8:1-2), and He will eventually establish His kingdom and seal Satan's defeat.

Episode 2: My Enemy, Your Enemy

CHAMPION Characteristics

Mental Toughness and Navigation

Power Verse: James 4:7-8A

Submit therefore to God. Resist the devil and he will flee from you. Draw near to God and He will draw near to you.

Story Summary

In this episode, Kratos, Teknon, and the mentors arrive on the planet Kairos, where they will carry out their mission. In the commercial market of the village of Kopto, Teknon makes an impulse purchase he later regrets. A skirmish occurs in which the team members use their unique weapons for the first time. Tor, Epps, Arti, and Matty are separated from Kratos and Teknon. Teknon and his father set up camp in the wooded outskirts of Kopto. Teknon learns from his father about the team's weapons and about Magos, the powerful enemy who is bent on destroying the societal values of Basileia. While building an army on Kairos, Magos sets a plan into motion that will lead to his domination of Basileia unless he is stopped. Kratos tells Teknon the origin of the CHAMPION Warriors and invites him to become a CHAMPION Warrior. He challenges Teknon to join him in the quest to defeat Magos and recover the Logos. Teknon accepts. At the close of the episode, Kratos coaches Teknon on the pitfalls of impulse spending.

Discussion Topics

Assess the enemy

Embrace your mission

Learn that God owns all things

Become an effective steward of your resources

Reconnaissance

1. Review the Map of the Mission on page 8 before beginning this section. Identify where the team is located in episode 2.

2. What is the CHAMPION definition of Mental Toughness? Of Navigation? (Refer to the CHAMPION Code on page 6.)

    Answer for Mental Toughness: "I will allow God to direct my thinking toward gaining common sense and wisdom. I will use discernment when making hard decisions. I will desire respect from others rather than compromise my convictions for acceptance or approval."

    Answer for Navigation: "I will allow God to chart my course by accepting my mission from Him, and I will complete that mission by trusting in Him. I will study the Bible, God's Word, so I can know Him better and gain His strength and direction for my life. I will become goal-oriented by learning to focus my attention on completing worthwhile short-term and long-term objectives."

There are times when obedient acts of self-sacrifice and courage merit both admiration and profound gratitude.

William Bennett

3. In this episode, Kratos describes the team's primary enemy. Who is he and why is he so dangerous? What is he trying to do?

   Answer: Magos is dangerous because he's brilliant and his objective is to destroy the moral and spiritual foundation of the people of Basileia. If he succeeds, the people will lose their ability to distinguish right from wrong and will forget their spiritual heritage. They will thus become more susceptible to tyrannical rule. Then, with the help of his android army, Magos plans to control and rule the planet.

4. What did Magos steal? Why did he steal it? Why did Kratos want to get it back?

   Answer: He stole the Logos to remove the only remaining archive of the CHAMPION Warriors and Pneuma's teachings from the people of Basileia. Kratos knew the importance of the Logos and its purpose as a beacon to point his people toward a relationship with Pneuma, as well as providing direction to live according to Pneuma's principles.

5. What is the CHAMPION definition of Ownership? (Refer to the CHAMPION Code on page 6.)

   Answer: "I will apply effective stewardship by using my life and the resources God entrusts to me—including my possessions, time, and talents—for His glory. I will seek contentment in God's provision for my needs. I will learn to practice delayed gratification."

QUESTION #4 TIP:

Emphasize how important God's Word (the Bible) is to us. We often take the availability of God's Word for granted. There are still countries in which the Bible is not available or is forbidden by the government. Just as Kratos sees the Logos as essential, so we should consider God's revealed Word as essential to our daily lives.

6. Why did Teknon buy the Shocktech?

   Answer: Because it looked sharp and felt good in his hand. He spent his money on emotion and then tried to justify his decision.

7. Did Teknon need the Shocktech? Why or why not?

   Answer: Teknon did not need it because his father and the mentors had already provided for his needs for protection and defense.

8a. Was Teknon free to spend his money the way he chose to spend it?

   Answer: Yes, it was Teknon's money and his father did not scold him for spending it.

8b. Was Teknon wise in the spending choice he made? Why?

   Answer: No, he made an impulsive purchase and did not take time to consider the implications of his purchase. One example of the lack of wisdom was that he used the majority of his money right at the beginning when it was set aside to cover expenses for his entire journey.

> *Nearly all men can stand adversity, but if you want to test a man's character, give him power.*
>
> Abraham Lincoln

9. What did Kratos recommend to Teknon about spending money?

   Answer: In order for him to spend wisely, not impulsively, Kratos gave three specific guidelines:

   Ask yourself if you really need it.

   Take time to think before making a purchase.

   Consider how much you have to spend and how to spend it wisely.

Strategy and Tactics

Who Is Your Enemy?

Did you know that the Bible says you have an enemy? And did you realize that you should hate this enemy and everything that he stands for? Your enemy is Satan, also known as the devil.

At one time, Satan was an angel, part of God's heavenly host (Isaiah 14:12-15, Luke 11:14-23).

But Satan became prideful and actually challenged God's authority. Like Magos, who chose to transform himself, Satan took matters into his own hands and allowed his pride to direct his actions. He wanted to become something he was not. He wanted to become God. As a result, God kicked him out of heaven forever.

When Satan was cast out, many of the other angels joined him in his rebellion. These angels now serve him around the world, which is currently in his control (1 John 5:19), by tempting, seducing, and enticing us to disobey God. Just like Scandalon is serving Magos, these angels serve Satan in his evil schemes.

Satan hates you and everything about you because he hates God. If you have invited Christ into your life, you are going to spend eternity with Christ in heaven. That is something Satan will never be able to do. Satan's mission is to ruin as many people as he can. He wants to accomplish his mission before Christ comes back again to rule forever.

1. Read 1 Peter 5:8. What does the Bible say that Satan wants to do to us?

   Answer: He wants to devour (ruin, destroy) us. We must realize that Satan is always at battle with us.

2. How should we respond to Satan's plan for us?

   Answer: Be self-controlled, sober in spirit, and alert. We need to make sure we are spending adequate time with the Lord to gain His direction, wisdom, and protection. We cannot let our guard down in any area where Satan could introduce temptation.

Satan wants to infect our thoughts, our desires, and our actions so that we will be ineffective for God. If you are a Christian, Satan can't prevent you from going to heaven, but he can make your life ineffective and miserable if you allow him to do so. What's worse, he will use your poor choices, ineffectiveness, and disobedience to display you as a poor example of God's sons to the world.

But there's good news! God knows that Satan is your enemy. Your Heavenly Father wants to provide all of the strength you need to defeat Satan every day. Through Jesus' death, burial, and resurrection, He has defeated the devil (Genesis 3:15) and has overcome the world (John 16:33). All you have to do is put your trust in Christ and obey His instructions to be victorious.

> *My message to you is: Be courageous! … Be as brave as your fathers before you. Have faith! Go forward.*
>
> Thomas A. Edison

✦ Session 1 ✦

Important Note:

Encourage your son to continue facing his fears. During this and future CHAMPION Sessions, encourage him to identify his fears one by one, and help him devise ways to overcome them on a regular basis. In effect, you will be teaching him to be a "Dolios Slayer." Teknon, at the end of his journey, will face Dolios, a creature who has the ability to transform himself into that which his opponent fears the most.

Important Note:

Another key element in spiritual warfare is putting on the "full armor of God" (Ephesians 6). You will discuss this topic with your son in a later session.

Defeat the Enemy

3. Read James 4:7-8. What does the Bible say to do to the devil to make him flee from you?

   Answer: First, submit to God. Then resist Satan and his temptations. You must cleanse your hands (actions) and purify your heart (thoughts, attitudes, willful desires). He will help you if you draw near to Him.

4. Why is it important for us to admit that Satan has influence in this world?

   Answer: We need to recognize that we have an enemy and become aware of his schemes and tactics.

5. Should we fear Satan? Why or why not?

   Answer: No, but we must learn his strategies and always be on the alert.

The Bible also says, "Greater is He [Christ] who is in you than he who is in the world [Satan]." You must realize that Satan is a formidable enemy, but you do not need to fear him. If you are a Christian, you belong to Almighty God, so He will give you guidance and protection. God also assigns His angels to us; they are charged with guarding those who fear and follow Him (Psalm 34:7, 91:11).

6. What can you do to protect yourself according to God's instructions in Psalm 119:9-11?

   Answer:

   (1) Stay pure by living according to God's Word.

   (2) Seek God with all your heart. According to Jesus in Mark 12:30, the greatest commandment is to "... love the Lord your God with all your heart, and with all your soul, and with all your mind, and with all your strength."

(3) Continue pursuing a strong relationship with the Lord.

(4) Treasure and store up His Word in your heart—read, study, and memorize it.

Effective Stewardship

7. Is it wrong to spend money? Absolutely not, but God wants us to spend it wisely. Did you know there are more verses in the Bible concerning money than on almost any other subject? Why do you think there are so many verses about money?

    Answer: Because money is such big part of our lives. How we handle money is an outward reflection of our inner beliefs and convictions. It has been said that if you want to see what's important to a man, look at his calendar and his checkbook.

Money is a tool God has given each of us to use and to manage. The way you manage money often reflects what you think about who provided it to you. Managing money is a visible expression of your relationship with God—your values and your trust in Him.

God is the owner of all good and perfect things on this earth. We are His stewards. What a privilege we have to be entrusted by God with His resources! God doesn't mind if you spend money. He may not even mind if you occasionally spend money on something you really want that you really don't need. But that should be the exception, not the rule.

Remember, God owns it all—our time, our talent, our possessions, and our money. He entrusts them to us. Think about what you buy before you buy it. Don't buy on the spur of the moment. Think and pray for wisdom before you make a big purchase. Seek wise counsel from others who are good stewards.

Have I not commanded you? Be strong and courageous! Do not tremble or be dismayed, for the Lord your God is with you wherever you go.

Joshua 1:9

When prosperity comes, do not use all of it.

Benjamin Franklin

Quote Tip:

Benjamin Franklin, one of the United States founding fathers, was himself a wealthy man. Franklin knew the value of saving and using resources wisely.

Ask your son this question: "Why is it important for you to start saving?"

Beware of little expenses. A small leak will sink a great ship.

Benjamin Franklin

♦ Session 1 ♦

QUESTION #8 TIP:

Even at this age, your son can begin to be a good steward. He can begin the process of tithing, saving, and spending wisely.

8. How can you become a good steward of your money and possessions?

MAIN THING:

Help your son by suggesting some key truths that he should have learned during this session, such as submitting to God, overcoming temptation, and understanding and resisting Satan's schemes.

THE MAIN THING I LEARNED FROM
EPISODE 2:

_____

_____

_____

_____

_____

Session 2: Episodes 3 and 4 of Teknon and the Champion Warriors

Episode 3: The Second Look

Champion Characteristic

Purity

Power Verse: 1 Corinthians 6:18

Flee immorality. Every other sin that a man commits is outside the body, but the immoral man sins against his own body.

Story Summary

In this episode, Magos sends Scandalon, a synthoid, to assume the form of an attractive young woman in order to tempt Teknon. Her name, Apoplanao (Lana), in the Greek language means "seducer." Teknon is both confused and enticed by the temptation and begins to make wrong choices based on his physical attraction to Lana. Later, he realizes he has been deceived. Kratos discusses the importance of sexual purity and offers guidelines to prepare against failure in this area. Kratos also proposes a somewhat radical approach toward setting boundaries in physical intimacy known as the Wedding Kiss.

Episode 3 Overview:

Establishing physical boundaries within relationships with the opposite sex and maintaining sexual purity before marriage are important topics, yet they can be difficult for a father and son to discuss. Teknon's temptation and decisions by the spring-fed pool, plus the wisdom shared by Kratos, will give both of you a natural opportunity to explore these important aspects of life. Consider using this opportunity to tell your son about sexual seduction and why it's important to avoid the temptations of an aggressive young woman. Also, challenge him to avoid being physically aggressive with young ladies and to respect and protect their purity as well.

Discussion Topics

Understanding the right context for sex
Establishing boundaries in physical intimacy
Setting high standards to guard your purity

Reconnaissance

1. Recite as much as you can of the CHAMPION Warrior Creed from memory (see page 5).

2. Review the Map of the Mission on page 8 and determine the team's location in episode 3.

3. What is the CHAMPION definition of **Purity**? (Refer to the CHAMPION Code on page 6.)

   Answer: "I will train myself to keep the temple of my body and mind uncorrupted mentally, emotionally, and physically. I will commit to avoid and flee sexual temptation."

4. Why do you think Scandalon tempted Teknon?

   Answer: In order to cause Teknon to suffer failure, experience guilt, and ultimately to destroy his character so that he would cause grief to Kratos and to Pneuma.

5. When should Teknon have returned to camp? Why?

   Answer: He should have returned to camp as soon as he realized there was a nearly naked woman in the pool. This would have prevented the possibility that he could be tempted to sin in his mind or body. Whether a girl has good intentions or is trying to ensnare you, lust is always a trap.

6. What did Teknon mean when he said, "I guess I shouldn't have taken the second look"?

   Answer: Instead of turning away from the young woman in the pool after he first saw her, Teknon hesitated and allowed himself to become more visually enticed. By taking the second look, he became tempted to sin in his mind.

7. What did Kratos mean when he said, "Error increases with distance"?

   Answer: Most failures in the sexual arena begin with a series of bad choices. Bad decisions, however small, will set us off from God's course and can lead to bigger mistakes and ultimately to serious failure.

8. How does that insight relate to physical and sexual intimacy?

   Answer: Physical closeness, even holding hands and kissing, can and will naturally lead to deeper levels of intimacy. This natural progression will only be stopped by making a proactive effort to stay on the course to purity.

9. Why do you think Kratos suggested that Teknon wait until marriage to kiss a woman?

   Answer: Kratos was trying to communicate that physical involvement naturally increases emotional involvement and commitment. He was encouraging Teknon to avoid

Important Caution:

By the time your son has reached between 8-10 years of age, chances are he is either hearing a description of sex from his peers or he is hearing the correct description and context from you. If you haven't already discussed sex with him, this may be an appropriate time to set this session aside and first explain the body changes he will experience (or is experiencing) in puberty, as well as the biological aspects of sex. For helpful resources, contact Generations of Virtue at www.generationsofvirtue.org or visit your local Christian retailer. As you proceed together through the discussion questions, allow adequate time for discussion. Give your son time to describe what is going on in his mind at this stage in his life.

✦ Session 2 ✦

unnecessary hurt or premature commitment with a young woman. Most important, he was challenging Teknon to set a high standard in the area of purity.

10. How did Teknon react to the idea of the Wedding Kiss?

Answer: He was interested, but uncertain as to whether he was willing to make such an extreme commitment.

> **QUESTION #2 TIP:**
>
> Scandalon changes into an attractive young woman in episode 3 in order to tempt Teknon. "Her" name is Apoplanao, which in Greek means "to seduce" or "seducer." Warn your son about sexual seduction, and reinforce why he should avoid the seductive temptations of an aggressive young woman, either in person or in pornographic materials. The Bible refers to temptations as "bait" that will hook you like a hungry fish. Pornography is another form of sexual bait; you will discuss this specifically in session 4.

STRATEGY AND TACTICS

1. Read 2 Corinthians 10:3-5. How can we win the battle for purity in our minds and hearts?

   Answer: By taking every thought captive to the obedience of Christ. To do this, you need to (1) know His commands by reading and studying the Bible, (2) ask Him on a daily basis to control your thoughts, and (3) pay attention to every thought, grab it, and make sure it is acceptable to God.

2. Read Romans 6:12-13. What does God say we should not do with our bodies?

   Answer: Do not present or offer parts of your body to sin, as instruments of wickedness (unrighteousness).

3. What does He say we should do with our bodies?

   Answer: Offer ourselves totally to God as an instrument of righteousness.

> *It's hard to beat a person who never gives up.*
>
> Babe Ruth

Just as Scandalon tempted Teknon, your enemy—Satan—wants to tempt you to fail in the area of sexual purity. If he can destroy your character, you are no longer a threat to him. Satan often uses sex to tempt us to sin. He sets traps for us and, if we don't allow God to control our desires, we'll walk right into them.

4. What does the Bible say about temptation in 1 Corinthians 10:13? How much can we depend on God when we are tempted?

> Answer: No temptation we experience is unique to us. Other men struggle in the same areas. God will not allow you to be tempted beyond what you are able to endure if you depend on Him. He is always faithful to provide a way to escape so that you can endure the test of your character.

God promises to provide a way out during any temptation we face. It may mean that we shouldn't take the second look. It will probably mean getting out of the tempting situation as quickly as possible. Remember, God promises to provide the power for you to live a pure life.

THE WEDDING KISS

Radical idea, right? But why not take every precaution possible to make sure that you will have the most fulfilling and intimate life possible with the wife God may eventually bring into your life? The world's approach to sex is not about creating more exciting and satisfying relationships, although the movie and music industry would try to tell us otherwise.

> *Let us not lose heart in doing good, for in due time we will reap if we do not grow weary. So then, while we have opportunity, let us do good to all people, and especially to those who are of the household of the faith.*
>
> Galatians 6:9-10

> *I have been crucified with Christ; and it is no longer I who live, but Christ lives in me; and the life which I now live in the flesh I live by faith in the Son of God, who loved me and gave Himself up for me.*
>
> Galatians 2:20

◆ SESSION 2 ◆

Sure the Wedding Kiss challenge sounds weird, but it's worth waiting for the benefits you'll receive in the long run. Kratos said that he wished someone had challenged him to meet such a goal. There are probably many men today who wish they had received a challenge like this when they were your age.

5. Read 1 Thessalonians 4:1-5. How do the Gentiles (non- Christians) behave regarding sexual activity?

   Answer: They follow their lustful passions and engage in sexual activity whenever they want to, thinking only of themselves.

6. How does God say He wants you to behave in this area?

   Answer: You should do everything to please God. You must be set apart (different) from the world.

The idea of the Wedding Kiss is a brave and bold commitment to purity. It's holding on to the precious gift of your body and emotions until you can give that gift to one special person. People who choose to refrain from sexual intimacy before marriage will be blessed by God in powerful ways.

7. What do you think your friends would think about the idea of the Wedding Kiss? How far do you think most teens will go physically with a girl?

8. Whether you go for the Wedding Kiss or not, you need to decide in advance how far you will go emotionally and physically with a girl before you are married. Have you ever really thought about how far you plan to go?

Dear brothers, you are only visitors here. Since your real home is in heaven I beg you to keep away from the evil pleasures of this world; they are not for you, for they wage war against your very soul.

1 Peter 2:11 (TLB)

Walk by the Spirit, and you will not carry out the desire of the flesh.

Galatians 5:16b

You may have already taken a few steps toward the cliff that Kratos talked about. You may have kissed a girl, or maybe become even more physically and emotionally involved with her. If you have, now is the time to confess this to God and seek His forgiveness. Then, recommit yourself to a higher standard. Claim God's promise of forgiveness and cleansing (1 John 1:9), and start fresh today in this area of purity.

MAIN THINGS:

If needed, help your son by suggesting some key truths that he should have learned during this session, such as establishing boundaries, fleeing temptation, setting high moral standards, and the Wedding Kiss.

THE MAIN THING I LEARNED FROM EPISODE 3:

_____

_____

_____

_____

♦ SESSION 2 ♦

EPISODE 4 OVERVIEW:

You'll be able to discuss with your son the importance of using good judgment when choosing friends—and having the integrity to stand for what's right. Today, peer pressure plays an important role in young people's lives. In addition to discussing Teknon's choices—and their consequences—you and your son will explore the wisdom that God gives to people who have placed their personal faith in Jesus Christ and seek to know Him better through Bible reading and prayer.

It's not whether you get knocked down, it's whether you get up.

Vince Lombardi

Episode 4 – The Company I Keep

Champion Characteristics

Mental Toughness and Integrity

Power Verse: 1 Corinthians 15:33

Do not be misled: Bad company corrupts good character. (NIV)

Story Summary

This episode finds Kratos and Teknon at the end of a week-long trek through a desolate forest. They are tired, hungry for "real" food, and ready for a change of pace. As they reach the city of Bia, which is known for its raucous nightlife and chaotic society, Kratos is hesitant to stop. Teknon, on the other hand, sees the bright lights, hears the sounds, and pictures the dinner delights awaiting them. Realizing that this is an opportune time for his son to learn more about discernment in decision-making, Kratos agrees to enter Bia. The Harpax, a local gang, provide the "classroom" for Teknon to learn his lesson the hard way.

Discussion Topics

Recognize the importance of discernment in choosing the right friends

Realize that there are always consequences to our choices

Recover from failure — part 1

Reconnaissance

1. Try to recite at least half of the CHAMPION Warrior Creed from memory (see page 5).
2. Review the Map of the Mission on page 8 and determine the team's location in episode 4.
3. What is the CHAMPION definition of **Mental Toughness**? Of **Integrity**? (Refer to the CHAMPION Code on page 6.)

    Answer for Mental Toughness: "I will allow God to direct my thinking toward gaining common sense and wisdom. I will use discernment when making hard decisions. I will desire respect from others rather than compromise my convictions for acceptance or approval."

    Answer for Integrity: "I will seek to acquire a clear understanding of who I am in Christ so that I may have a deeper comprehension of what I believe, what I stand for, and how I can live out those convictions in the most difficult circumstances, whether I am alone or with others. I will allow other people to hold me accountable to standards of excellence."

Hold yourself responsible for a higher standard than anybody else expects of you. Never excuse yourself.

Henry Ward Beecher

4a. Do you believe Teknon used good judgment in Bia? Why or why not?

> Answer: He became overly impressed with appearance rather than character. He did not choose his companions wisely.

4b. If not, at which moments in this episode did he show poor judgment?

> Answer: The first time was when he was willing to risk entering an unfavorable environment (Bia) to get a good night's sleep and a hot meal. He also decided to start a conversation with the Harpax instead of following his father's advice to get some rest. Later on, he did not leave the Harpax when he heard their vulgar speech and rebellious attitudes.

5. When should Teknon have realized that he should avoid the Harpax?

> Answer: When his dad encouraged him to get a good night's sleep instead of staying up late.

6. The leader of the Harpax is named Rhegma. The Greek word rhegma means "ruin." In what ways could a person like Rhegma ruin the life of a young man like Teknon?

> Answer: Rhegma is charismatic and attractive, but he is also evil. Teens can be drawn in by the physical appearance and popularity of people like Rhegma if they are not grounded in a relationship with Christ.

QUESTION #7 TIP:

Your son will learn more about the principle of "recovering" later in the CHAMPION Training.

7. What did Kratos mean when he said, "It's better to be trusted and respected than it is to be liked"?

> Answer: Kratos wanted to encourage Teknon that, although it's great to be liked, he can get into trouble by trying to

please others in order to be accepted. If acceptance is the goal, compromise soon follows. In the end, people who live by their convictions are respected and trusted by others.

8. Kratos also told Teknon that he must learn from his mistake and to recover. What does it mean to recover? How would you recover if you made a mistake like Teknon made?

   Answer: Kratos wanted Teknon to admit his mistakes, learn from them, and move ahead with his mission.

9. Kratos cautioned, "Observe all of the characteristics of a person." What characteristics should you watch for?

   Answer:

   GOOD Characteristics:

   ▲ Honesty
   ▲ Self-control (especially in speech and temper)
   ▲ Willingness to help others
   ▲ Respect of family members and others
   ▲ Desire to know God and obey Him

   BAD Characteristics:
   ▲ Dishonesty
   ▲ Bad temper
   ▲ Vulgar speech
   ▲ Disrespect of parents and others
   ▲ Lack of desire to develop his relationship with Christ or to obey God

Rather fail with honor than succeed by fraud.

Sophocles

Associate yourself with men of good quality if you esteem your own reputation; for it is better to be alone than in bad company.

George Washington

10. What do you think Kratos meant when he said, "Bad

humor is a sign of bad morals"?

Answer: Vulgar language and humor is rampant among teenagers today. Your son needs to understand that friends who use profanity and bad humor may have deeper spiritual problems.

Strategy and Tactics

Most of the book of Proverbs in the Old Testament was written by one of the wisest men who ever lived, King Solomon. In this book, Solomon instructed his sons and the young men of his kingdom about the difference between knowledge (having the facts) and wisdom (applying those facts to life). Like Teknon, young men can choose to reject the wisdom of their parents and the Word of God. As they grow older, however, they will increase their knowledge, but not their wisdom and discernment. In Proverbs 1, Solomon described the danger of being a young man who lacks discernment.

1a. Read Proverbs 1. What can a person do to begin obtaining wisdom? (See verses 7-9.)

Answer: First, he must revere (fear) God and study His teaching. Second, he must respect his parents' authority and guidance.

1b. What advice did Solomon give in verses 15 and 16 concerning the importance of choosing the right friends?

Answer: Do not go along with bad companions because they will drag you along into evil. Their way may seem attractive, but it leads to destruction.

1c. According to verses 23-27, why should we listen to sound advice and wisdom?

Answer: Because it will save us from bad choices that lead to ruin.

1d. What will happen if we don't obey God and use discernment? (See verses 28-32.)

Answer: If we ignore God's wisdom, He will allow us to suffer the negative consequences that we have brought on ourselves.

1e. What will happen if we use good judgment and listen to wisdom? (See verse 33.)

Answer: We will benefit (live securely) as a result of wise choices and decisions.

Always remember two things about your Heavenly Father: God loves you and He is trustworthy.

God loves you

Just as Kratos loved Teknon despite his bad decisions, so your Father in heaven loves you no matter what you do. He understands that you are growing and learning how to follow Him. Sometimes you will succeed, and sometimes you will fail. As you grow to know Him better and seek to obey His Word, you will increase in discernment and find it easier to make better choices.

But no matter how hard we try, we will still sin and disobey God. Romans 3:23 tells us that we have all sinned. God understands us and loves us so much that He sent Jesus to die on the cross and then raised Him again from the dead to pay for our sins (or failures). After we sin, we recover by confessing our failure to God and then claiming His promise of forgiveness. Then, we turn from our own way and go God's way. We should also apologize to anyone we have offended.

✦ Session 2 ✦

MAIN THINGS:

If needed, help your son by suggesting some key truths that he should have learned during this session, such as discernment in choosing friends, characteristics of a good friend, consequences of our choices, and recovering from failure.

2. What does 1 John 1:9 say about God and confessing our sins to Him? How does this make you feel?

   Answer: "If we confess our sins, He [God] is faithful and righteous to forgive us our sins and to cleanse us from all unrighteousness." If we confess, He promises to forgive us and totally cleanse us.

THE MAIN THING I LEARNED FROM EPISODE 4:

_____

_____

_____

_____

_____

Session 3: Episodes 5 and 6 of Teknon and the Champion Warriors

Episode 5: Ergonian Pride

Champion Characteristic

Attitude

Power Verse: Proverbs 19:20 (NIV)

Listen to advice and accept instruction, and in the end you will be wise.

Story Summary

In episode 5, Kratos and Teknon emerge from the jungles of Perasmos and enter the luxurious accommodations of the resort community of Ergo. Ergo enjoys an isolated existence on Kairos, surrounded by a high wall that only opens to the sea. Planning to meet the other team members in Ergo, Kratos and Teknon rent a room and meet the arrogant resort manager, Mr. Poroo, who ignores Kratos' warning about the threat of an attack by savage beasts called amachos. The beasts create havoc and hurt guests in Ergo. The resort is only saved when Kratos and Matty repel the amachos.

Episode 5 Overview:

In this session, you and your son will explore the importance of teachability. As Mr. Poroo illustrates, an arrogant person who refuses to listen to wise counsel will eventually suffer—or at least the people around him will. The book of Proverbs contains many verses that describe the wisdom of being teachable.

Your son will be challenged to recognize the value of listening to the counsel of his parents and, even more importantly, to his Heavenly Father, who has given us His words in the Bible.

When a man is wrapped up in himself, he makes a pretty small package.

John Ruskin

Discussion Topics

The danger of pride

The importance of a teachable attitude

Listen to wise counsel

Reconnaissance

1. Review the Map of the Mission on page 8 and determine the team's location in episode 5. Trace the steps the team has covered thus far. Review story highlights and main topics discussed.

2. What is the CHAMPION definition of **Attitude**? (Refer to the CHAMPION Code on page 6.)

    Answer: "I will cultivate a disposition of humility. I will assume a correct and hopeful view of myself as a member of God's family. I will improve my ability to manage anger and discouragement. I will develop and enjoy an appropriate sense of humor."

3. What kind of attitude did Mr. Poroo have toward Kratos? Why?

    Answer: Poroo displayed an attitude of arrogance, especially when Kratos recommended that the manager take precautions against the amachos.

4. What occurred as a result of Mr. Poroo's attitude?

    Answer: The amachos entered Ergo, caused a great deal of fear and destruction, and injured several guests.

5. What does the word "teachable" mean to you?

   Answer: One possible definition is the willingness to consider wise counsel and to change one's behavior as a result of that counsel. It also means that you are humble and open to learning new things.

Strategy and Tactics

Life would be much easier if we were teachable, wouldn't it?

1. What does Proverbs 19:20 say about being teachable?

   Answer: "Listen to counsel [advice] and accept discipline [consider instruction], that you may be wise the rest of your days."

2. What happens if you are not teachable? (Read Proverbs 29:1.)

   Answer: "A man who hardens his neck [remains stubborn and unchanged] after much reproof will suddenly be broken beyond remedy."

   Read Proverbs 16:18-19 and Proverbs 18:12.

Important Note:

Discuss your stand on alcohol with your son. Opinions of God's standard in this area vary. Regardless of your position, you can discuss the danger of using alcohol as an escape from reality and the ease of becoming addicted and enslaved to it. Also, share the clear biblical mandate from Ephesians 5:18: " ... do not get drunk with wine for it is dissipation, but be filled with the Spirit."

Teachability is a man's capacity for growth.

Howard Hendricks

✦ Session 3 ✦

Easy Mistakes:

Does your son respond well to instruction? Or does he bristle at even the implication of a helpful hint? This session focuses on several key issues concerning pride. Why, for instance, is it important to receive and apply the advice of godly, wise people? How can a prideful attitude get us into trouble? Ultimately, of course, pride is a spiritual issue because it results in a rebellious attitude toward God.

Question #4 Tip:

This question gives your son a third-party reference point to discuss teachability. It temporarily takes the focus from him so that he can discuss it objectively.

Question #5 Tip:

These verses highlight specific practical benefits of listening to the advice of parents, as well as to the Lord.

3a. What kind of attitude creates the greatest barrier to becoming teachable and leads to destruction in the end?

Answer: Pride, which the Bible also calls a "haughty spirit."

3b. What kind of attitude makes us teachable and leads to honor?

Answer: Humility. This does not mean that we have a poor opinion of ourselves, but rather that we don't think more highly of ourselves than we should, especially in relation to our awesome God.

God knows what is best for us. When we reject God's wisdom and direction in our decisions, we are trying to do His job. When we aren't teachable, we don't pay attention to God's Word. We also don't listen to people whom God puts into our lives to give us advice and counsel—like our parents, pastors, and teachers. We saw what happened to Mr. Poroo when he didn't listen to Kratos' advice. Make sure you are seeking God with a teachable heart so that He can reveal how to live your life for Him.

4. Do you think your friends (name a few) are teachable? Why or why not?

Read Proverbs 6:20-23

My son, observe the commandment of your father and do not forsake the teaching of your mother; bind them continually on your heart; tie them around your neck. When you walk about, they will guide you; when you sleep, they will watch over you; and when you awake, they will talk to you. For the commandment is a lamp, and the teaching is light; and reproofs for discipline are the way of life ...

5. What are the some of the benefits of listening to your parents?

```
┌─────────────────────────────────────────┐
│                                         │
│   THE MAIN THING I LEARNED FROM         │
│              EPISODE 5:                 │
│                                         │
│   _____   │
│                                         │
│   _____   │
│                                         │
│   _____   │
│                                         │
│   _____   │
│                                         │
│   _____   │
│                                         │
└─────────────────────────────────────────┘
```

IMPORTANT NOTE:

This would be a good time to highlight the importance of some spiritual disciplines for your son. Help him understand that by developing a habit of daily Bible study and prayer, he will see his relationship with God grow stronger, and he will become more teachable as a result. Encourage him to trust that God will prosper him in many ways as he pursues God in this way.

Success isn't forever, and failure isn't fatal.

Don Shula

MAIN THINGS:

If needed, help your son by suggesting some key truths that he should have learned during this session, such as the danger of pride, the importance of teachability, and seeking wise counsel.

Episode 6: A Storm of Dishonor

CHAMPION Characteristics

Honor and Attitude

Power Verse: Romans 12:10

Be devoted to one another in brotherly love; give preference to one another in honor.

Story Summary

In this episode Kratos and his team take to the seas, riding an elaborate luxury ship named the Ergonaut toward the city of Sarkinos. During the trip, Teknon meets two overindulged young men named Pikros and Parakoe, who constantly bicker, complain, and demonstrate a disrespect toward their father. Their disrespect helps Teknon to realize his own neglect in honoring his sister, Hilly.

Magos finally surfaces in this episode. He is a self-created cyborg, a former partner of Kratos, and the team's enemy. He can observe almost anything on Kairos from his fortress, through the eyes of his androids and transmission technology. Magos uses his technology to create a hurricane-force storm that hammers the Ergonaut and forces the team members to use all of their powers to save the ship and its passengers. During the storm, Teknon acts bravely to rescue the Pikros and Parakoe's father.

Episode 6 Overview:

In this session, you will have the opportunity to discuss with your son what it means to honor another person. You will talk about ways in which he can show honor to you, your spouse, siblings, and other people he meets.

Spend less time worrying who's right, and spend more time deciding what's right!

Life's Little Instruction Book

Discussion Topics:

Show respect to family members

Show honor to others — place value on people and communicate that value to them

Reconnaissance

1. Try to recite all of the CHAMPION Warrior Creed from memory (see page 5).

2. Review the Map of the Mission on page 8 and determine the team's location in episode 6.

3. What is the CHAMPION definition of **Honor**? Of **Attitude**? (Refer to the CHAMPION Code on page 6.)

    Answer for Honor: "I will honor God by obeying Him and acknowledging Him as the complete source of my life, both now and through eternity. I will treat my parents, brothers/sisters, friends, and acquaintances with respect. I will appreciate the strengths and accept the weaknesses of all my 'team members.'"

    Answer for Attitude: "I will cultivate a disposition of humility. I will assume a correct and hopeful view of myself as a member of God's family. I will improve my ability to manage anger and discouragement. I will develop and enjoy an appropriate sense of humor."

4. How did Pikros and Parakoe treat their father? What did they reveal about their relationship with him?

    Answer: The brothers showed a complete lack of respect for their father.

QUESTION #1 TIP:

By this time, your son should able to recite the CHAMPION Warrior Creed. God will use this and his memory verses to direct his thinking. This creed will also be an effective passage for him to recite during his celebration at the completion of his training.

Kind words do not cost much ... yet they accomplish much.

Blaise Pascal

♦ Session 3 ♦

The deepest principle in human nature is the craving to be appreciated.

William James

5. How did Pikros and Parakoe treat each other?

   Answer: With impatience, anger, and selfishness.

6. How did Teknon feel as he observed the boys' attitudes toward their father? Why did he feel this way?

   Answer: He was disturbed by their attitudes. Because Teknon had been raised to exhibit love and respect for Kratos, he could not imagine treating his father in such a manner.

7. How did watching Pikros and Parakoe affect Teknon's attitude toward his sister Hilly?

   Answer: Teknon recognized he needed to show more honor to his sister.

8. Do you think Teknon shows respect toward his father and mother? Why do you think so?

   Answer: Help your son identify examples in the story when Teknon, by his speech and actions, has shown respect for Kratos and Paideia (there are examples near the end of episodes 2, 3, and 4). Even though he has made some bad decisions, Teknon does listen to his parents' counsel. As a family, they have actively worked at relationships and character development.

Strategy and Tactics

An Honorable Attitude

Read Exodus 20:12. This is one of the Ten Commandments.

1a. What does this commandment say about the attitude young people should have toward their parents?

Answer: Honor your father and mother.

1b. What does God promise the results will be if we obey His commandment?

Answer: He promises that you will "live long in the land the Lord your God has given you." In other words, He promises that your life will go better and that you will live a long, full life. (See also Ephesians 6:1-3 where Paul quotes these words.)

2. What are some practical ways in which you can show honor to your parents?

Some examples include:

▲ Speak respectfully of your parents when you are not with them.

▲ Obey them quickly and with a good attitude when they ask you to do something.

3. What does Galatians 6:9-10 say about how young people should treat their brothers and sisters?

Answer: They should not grow weary in treating siblings well. Over time, treating siblings with respect will cause them and us to mature; it will "reap a harvest" in all of our lives. God says that we should be especially kind and loving to

An Honorable Attitude:

We, as fathers, need to communicate and model for our sons what it means to show respect and esteem to the people that God brings into our lives.

Most of us, swimming against the tides of trouble the world knows nothing about, need only a bit of praise or encouragement – and we'll make the goal.

Jerome P. Fleishman

◆ Session 3 ◆

IMPORTANT NOTE:

Some of the boys going through this study probably have some difficult situations in their families. Assure them that God always loves them, even in tough times. Encourage them that God promises to work ALL things (even the bad stuff) for good for those that love Him (Romans 8:28). If there are significant issues with your young man's (or young men's) family, consult your pastor or a trained Christian counselor.

other Christians and our own family members.

4. Read Romans 12:10. How can we "do good" within our family?

   Answer: Be devoted to each other and give preference to others. This means setting aside our own desires and serving others as Jesus did throughout his life. God calls husbands to be servant-leaders (Ephesians 5:25), which requires giving up your own desires and giving others preference. True leaders are unselfish servants.

The Bible says we ought to "do good to all people." That should especially apply to our family members.

5. How do you view your parents? How about your brothers and sisters? Do you act like Pikros and Parakoe? Or do you view your family, even with their flaws, as valuable people given to you by God?

The members of your family are valuable gifts that God has given you. Are they always easy to get along with? No way! Are you?

Does what they do always make sense? Absolutely not! Does what you do always make sense? Enough said.

A CHAMPION strives to maintain the right attitudes, no matter what other people do. Read Genesis 37:18-36. Joseph's brothers sold him into slavery because they were jealous of him. Even though his capture was a terrible thing, God used Joseph's captivity in an awesome way to eventually place Joseph as the second most powerful man in the Egyptian empire.

Read Genesis 45 to see how Joseph forgave his brothers even when he had the power to hurt them. Joseph understood that "God causes all things to work together for good to those who love God, to those who are called according to His purpose" (see Romans 8:28b).

6. If your brother or sister doesn't show you honor, what should you do?

   Answer: Show honor and respect to them anyway.

7. Why should you respond this way?

   Answer: Because God loves them and us no matter what we do. God tells us to love and forgive others, just as He loves and forgives us. If you persist in love, you will reap a "good harvest" in your life and their life as well.

   You should honor your parents as God's chosen authority in your life. If you have any brothers and sisters, you should honor them as treasured co-workers and help your family to become all that God wants it to be. Don't end up like Pikros and Parakoe. Remember, you honor God by the way you treat other people.

   Take steps as a CHAMPION to maintain the right *Attitude* and show *Honor* to your family.

8. What are some practical ways you can you show honor to your mother? How about your brothers and sisters?

Remember the three R's: Respect for self, Respect for others, and Responsibility for your actions.

Life's Little Instruction Book II

A man's wisdom gives him patience; it is to his glory to overlook an offense.

Proverbs 19:11 (NIV)

Main Things:

If needed, help your son by suggesting some key truths that he should have learned during this session, like the importance of honoring others, especially family members.

The Main Thing I Learned from Episode 6:

_____

_____

_____

_____

_____

Session 4: Episodes 7 and 8 of Teknon and the Champion Warriors

Episode 7: An Excellent Choice

Champion Characteristics

Purity and Integrity

Power Verse: Psalm 101:3

I will set no worthless thing before my eyes; I hate the work [deeds] of those who fall away; it shall not fasten its grip on me.

Story Summary

    This episode opens with Kratos and his team disembarking the Ergonaut and entering the seductive, underworld community of Sarkinos. They hope to link up with an informant, Pseudes, who will provide strategic information vital to the team's battle plan.
    Sarkinos supports an elaborate, highly technical "red-light" district. Holographic imaging salons abound throughout this section of the city, offering interactive pornography to the paying public. Teknon disobeys his father's instruction to remain in the hotel room and follows Psuedes, who is plotting an attack on the team. Teknon soon finds himself in the center of the red-light district, where he faces a new type of temptation.

Episode 7 Overview:

Discuss with your son the importance of developing a game plan for what material he will and will not allow to enter the window of his mind. This includes movies, videos, DVDs, TV, music, reading material, videogames, and especially the Internet. Viewing pornographic material will distort how a man perceives and responds to women. For many men the lure of pornography becomes addictive.

The second issue you should cover at the end of this session OR at a separate meeting is masturbation. Many guys struggle with masturbation at times in their lives, so why not help your son learn to deal with this temptation as soon as possible?

Question #1 Tip:

For a change, you should take the initiative to recite the CHAMPION Warrior Creed to set an example for your son.

Teknon is coerced to enter an imaging salon by Eros, the salon host. Teknon wisely recognizes the evil and leaves. He meets up with Arti and Epps, and together they capture Pseudes and take him back to the hotel for interrogation. As the episode closes, Teknon confesses that he made a poor decision in disobeying his father, but he is praised because he made the right choice to flee the temptation of pornography in the salon.

Discussion Topics

Protect your mind from inappropriate material

Avoid temptation

Run from temptation

Establish your convictions in advance

Reconnaissance

1. Recite all of the CHAMPION Warrior Creed from memory (see page 5).

2. Review the Map of the Mission on page 8 before beginning this section. Identify where the team is located in episode 7.

3. Review the CHAMPION definition of **Purity** and of **Integrity** (refer to the CHAMPION Code on page 6.)

   Answer for Purity: "I will train myself to keep the temple of my body and mind uncorrupted mentally, emotionally, and physically. I will commit to avoid and flee sexual temptation."

   Answer for Integrity: "I will seek to acquire a clear understanding of who I am in Christ so that I may have a deeper comprehension of what I believe, what I stand for, and how I can live out those convictions in the most difficult circumstances, whether I am alone or with others. I will allow other people to hold me accountable to standards of excellence."

Important Note:

Emphasize the importance of making the decision to avoid temptations by completely avoiding compromising situations, if at all possible.

4. What did Eros try to get Teknon to do? Why?

   Answer: Eros tried to get him to see images of naked women. Eros knew that if Teknon started watching the sexual images, he would stay and see more. If Teknon stayed, Eros would make money through tempting him with a free look.

5. Why do you think Teknon chose not to stay in the image salon?

   Answer: Teknon immediately sensed the danger of the situation. Based on his father's example and instruction, he knew that the conditions within the imaging salon did not align with his father's values.

6. What did Kratos say about the effect of pornography?

   Answer: The images degrade women and give a false and sinful perspective on sexual intimacy. Pornographic images burn themselves into the memory of those who choose to view them.

7. Why were Kratos and the mentors so excited about Teknon's decision to leave the imaging salon?

   Answer: Because he made the right choice when faced with a serious temptation. He practiced discernment and self-control.

✦ Session 4 ✦

8. Even though Teknon made an excellent choice at the imaging salon, when did he make a bad choice?

   Answer: Teknon made a bad choice when he left the hotel room and disobeyed his father. By attempting to track Pseudes, Teknon put himself in the vulnerable position to be exposed to pornographic images in the salons. Even if Teknon's decision was for a good cause, it did not justify his disobedience. Partial obedience is still disobedience.

   Epps helped Teknon to see the danger that surrounded him when he said, "You [Teknon] took a big chance when you decided to go out on your own and walk past those places. All of us are tempted to look at bad material like that, but we can't afford to take those kinds of risks. We've got to stay as far away from them as possible."

Strategy and Tactics

1. What are some of the sources of pornography in our society? (Hint: Think about what you see and hear.)

   Answer: The Internet, movies, videos, TV, some video games, magazines/books.

2. What do you think pornography does to a person's mind?

   Answer: It distorts the true picture of God's gift of sex for oneness and enjoyment in marriage. It also creates a desire to see more and increasingly explicit images. Watching pornography can easily become an addiction that hard wires our brain to crave the imagery. In effect, it creates an addiction that damages us spiritually as we focus our minds on sexual fantasy and shut ourselves off from a relationship with God.

Our minds act like computers and cameras. Just as a computer's response is based on the data programmed into it, whatever data we put into our minds will affect how we view the world and how we respond to it. It's not quite this simple because our minds are far more complex than any computer in the world, but the basic principles work the same way.

You have probably heard the phrase, "garbage in, garbage out." When we allow ourselves to view sexually explicit material, it's like downloading a computer virus into the hard-drive of our minds. Those images start to corrupt our thinking and how we react to other people.

Our minds are also like a camera because, when we look at a pornographic picture or video, our minds record it—and store it to be brought back again and again.

Failure to prepare is preparing to fail.

John Wooden

3a. What does Romans 12:2 mean by "do not be conformed to this world"?

Answer: J.B. Phillips translates these words as "don't let the world around you squeeze you into its own mold". We either conform ourselves to the world's mold or we conform to the mold of Jesus Christ that we see through God's Word and the empowering of the Holy Spirit.

3b. What do you think "renewing of your mind" means?

Answer: The Greek word for transform is the root word that we derive the word "morph" from. God wants to morph us, to change us. Morphing comes from the inside out. Our thinking is greatly shaped by our family and our culture. In order to be conformed to the image or mold of Jesus, our way of thinking and of viewing the world needs to be renewed or remolded to line up with God's perspectives. We must trust God, study His Word, and pray on a regular basis. God remolds our thinking throughout our life.

QUOTE TIP:

John Wooden is the most successful college basketball coach of all time. When he coached he was committed to train and prepare players to be the best they could be.

Ask your son: "Why is preparation ahead of time so important to making right decisions?"

Use this question to reinforce the need of thinking through media boundaries ahead of time so that we don't make wrong choices when opportunities present themselves.

✦ Session 4 ✦

> *Do not offer the parts of your body to sin, as instruments of wickedness, but rather offer yourselves to God, as those who have been brought from death to life; and offer the parts of your body to Him as instruments of righteousness.*
>
> Romans 6:13 (NIV)

PHIL 4:8 STANDARD:

Encourage your son not only to avoid the "bad stuff," but also to seek out the "good stuff." Media that meets the "PHIL 4:8" standard can have a strong influence for good in his life. As a parent, you should preview movies or read reviews and screen movies to protect your children.

As we choose to draw near to God and yield our lives to the power of His Holy Spirit, He will give us the power NOT to conform to this world. As we allow God to reshape our defective thinking to align with His mind, our attitudes and actions will change. Life-change occurs from the inside out.

4. What do you think this phrase means: "let us throw off everything that hinders and the sin that so easily entangles" (Hebrews 12:1b NIV)?

   Answer: If we want to win a race, we have to ditch the things in our lives can either be (1) distractions from our goals or (2) sins that trip us up.

5. Have any of your friends asked you to look at pornography? How did you respond?

6. According to Psalm 101:3, what should your stand be on pornography or any explicit images that tempt you?

   Answer: To hate those hindrances that weigh us down in the race of life and to set no worthless or vile thing before our eyes so that it will not take hold.

7. What does God promise to offer you if you are willing to trust Him when you face a temptation (read 1 Corinthians 10:13)?

   Answer: God is faithful. He will ALWAYS provide a way of escape in a temptation. We will be tempted, but we don't have to walk into a trap. God will always give us a way out, but we must choose to take His escape route. We have to work with God to retrain our minds so that we come to hate those things that drag us down. Then we must take God's escape route every time out of temptation. IF we don't move quickly toward the escape hatch, we will be likely to get sucked into the trap!

Hoplon is a Greek term that refers to armor or weapons of warfare. Just as Teknon and Kratos need their armor to protect them in the battle, Christians also need armor — spiritual armor. The Bible describes this armor of God in Ephesians 6:10-18.

8. What makes up the spiritual armor that God provides for us? How could this armor help you to gain more self-discipline in what you watch, listen to, and read?

    Answer:

    ▲ Belt of truth (our integrity and honesty)

    ▲ Breast plate of righteousness (doing the right things in obedience to God)

    ▲ Shoes of readiness (being fully trained)

    ▲ Shield of faith (our trust in God no matter what is fired our way)

    ▲ Helmet of salvation (our salvation through Jesus Christ will guard our minds)

    ▲ Sword of the Spirit (the Word of God—the Bible is our only offensive weapon)

These physical objects are metaphors representing God's gifts of protection and spiritual weapons that will help us in the battle against temptation. We need to put on God's full armor or we will not be ready to do battle with Satan. We must trust God and make the right choices in what we see, think, and do.

Important Note:

This would be a good time to help your son to get used to the concept of having an accountability partner. Let him know that you are his accountability partner during his CHAMPION Training, but that in the future he should set up an accountability partner or small group.

Later … help your son find a strong partner or develop a small group with a few young men for accountability. When it's time, suggest that as accountability partners, the guys should meet regularly to share issues, pray for each other, and specifically ask each other about this area of purity and other areas of growth and commitment. Just as they are for you, ongoing accountability and support are very important for your son.

◆ Session 4 ◆

Your Boundaries:

Be ready to discuss what your boundaries are in these areas—and why these boundaries are so important. Some fathers, for example, agree not to watch anything that they would not want their kids to watch.

I do not pray for success. I ask for faithfulness.

Mother Teresa

When you put on the armor of God, it's almost like Kratos putting on the Hoplon. God gives you all of the weapons you need to fight your enemy, Satan. Satan would like nothing more than for you to start a habit of looking at pornographic or sensual material so that your relationship with God and other people will be hindered.

9. What do you think are some of the benefits of not looking at pornography?

    Answer: A clean mind, more self-control, no guilty feelings, a pure relationship with your future wife, and a closer relationship with God are just a few benefits of using self-discipline concerning porn.

Setting high standards for what you watch, read, and listen to is a lot like racing toward that cliff Kratos described a few episodes ago. The best time to put on the brakes is when you know the cliff is ahead. The danger from pornography, like the cliff, is ahead. Decide to put on your brakes now by refusing to look at any pornography. Ask your father or mother, and one of your trusted Christian friends, to pray for you and make sure you are holding the line in this area.

Take heart if you have already failed or even developed a bad habit in this area. Remember that God loves you and is waiting for you to seek His forgiveness. Don't let the guilt that so often comes with this habit overtake you and make you depressed. You can restore fellowship with God today and draw on His strength to help you kick the habit. Jesus said, "I have overcome the world" (John 16:33). Since He has overcome the world, He can help you overcome your habits and tendencies. Be courageous enough to share your difficulties with your father today and ask him to help you.

The Main Thing I Learned from Episode 7:

_____

_____

_____

_____

_____

Main Things:

If needed, help your son by suggesting some key truths that he should have learned during this session, such as the importance of deciding standards in advance, setting high standards, good media vs. bad media (the PHIL 4:8 test), and fleeing temptation.

Episode 8 Overview:

In this session, you have the opportunity to help your son distinguish between successful failure, and unsuccessful failure. In successful failure, you persevere under difficult circumstances after you fail to accomplish a worthwhile task, and then you manage to recover from that failure and try again. In unsuccessful failure, you face the same situation and don't put forth your all, thus giving up or only partially achieving your potential.

Unsuccessful failure is usually the result of bad choices or disobedience to God. Your son needs to know the difference between successful and unsuccessful failure, and understand that he can experience successful failures in his life.

Episode 8: Faced with Fear

CHAMPION Characteristic

Courage

Power Verse: Joshua 1:9 (NIV)

Have I not commanded you? Be strong and courageous. Do not be terrified; do not be discouraged, for the Lord your God will be with you wherever you go.

Story Summary

After leaving Sarkinos, the CHAMPION team resumes its search for their informant by hiking toward a small mining village. A band of Magos' footsoldiers ambushes them on the trail. All the combined powers of the team members are required to win the brief, but fierce, battle. Teknon hides during a crucial moment of the battle and then blames himself for shrinking away when he was afraid. He believes he failed his team members when they needed him most.

After the battle is over, a figure suddenly appears from the darkness, unnoticed. Scandalon, an android from Magos' elite fighting force called the Kakos, surrounds the team with a dangerous energy field that will vaporize them within an hour. Only Teknon escapes, and therefore must assume responsibility for rescuing his companions. Because of his earlier response to the footsoldiers, Teknon shrinks in fear from such a daunting task. The episode ends with Kratos telling Teknon that he is their only hope for survival.

Discussion Topics

**Overcoming fear of rejection fear of failure
Learning to recover from failure**

Optional Exercise: Watch the movie "Apollo 13" together

Apollo 13 is an excellent film that describes a true story about facing fear and emerging victorious in what the primary person in the film, Jim Lovell, describes as a "successful failure."

Reconnaissance

1. Review the Map of the Mission on page 8 and determine the team's location in episode 8.

2. Review the CHAMPION definition of **Courage**. (Refer to the CHAMPION Code on page 6.)

    Answer: "I will cultivate bravery and trust in God. I will break out of my comfort zone by seeking to conquer my fears. I will learn to recover, recover, and recover again."

3. What happened to Teknon during the team's fight with the footsoldiers?

    Answer: When the footsoldiers attacked, Teknon froze. Kratos got hurt while protecting Teknon during the attack.

The credit belongs to the man who is actually in the arena; whose face is marred by dust and sweat and blood; who strives valiantly; who errs and comes up short again and again; who knows the great enthusiasms, the great devotions, and spends himself in a worthy cause; who at the best knows in the end the triumph of high achievement; and who at the worst, if he fails, at least fails while daring greatly ...

Theodore Roosevelt

Quote Tip:

Ask your son why President Roosevelt said the credit belongs to the man who is actually in the arena. Answer: We learn and achieve by stepping out. Only those who step forward to take risks by faith, trusting God to provide the strength and resources for accomplishing great things ... will receive the satisfaction and reward God intended.

4. Why do you think Teknon responded the way he did during the battle?

   Answer: He allowed his fear to control him.

5. How did Teknon feel about his performance during the battle? Why?

   Answer: He felt embarrassed and guilty. He felt that he had let his team down by deserting them while they were courageously protecting him in the battle.

6. Epps also coached Teknon that, "You learn by doing." How does this apply to Teknon?

   Answer: As Teknon takes risks and tries new things, he may initially fail, but if he presses on and continues to try, he will learn and begin a lifelong process of mastering different areas of his life.

In great attempts, it is glorious even to fail.

Vince Lombardi

If we confess our sins, He [God] is faithful and righteous to forgive us our sins and to cleanse us from all unrighteousness.

1 John 1:9

Strategy and Tactics

The size of a person is determined by what it takes to stop him. – Dr. Howard Hendricks

Failure has two faces. There are successful failures, and there are unsuccessful failures. *Apollo 13* was a successful failure. Not only did the astronauts return home safely under incredibly difficult circumstances, they also exercised a high level of creative output and genuine teamwork over a period of only five days that rivals any single human endeavor of the century.

Learning to Recover

Dave Simmons, former linebacker of the Dallas Cowboys, had an interesting football philosophy that applies to the rest of life too. He said, "Every play is a game; learn to recover, recover, recover."

Simmons explained in his seminar *Dad the Family Shepherd* that every play during a football game is like a game in itself. The team plans for the play, gets information for the play, and then executes the play. Usually the play is a success. Sometimes it's not. Whether or not the play is successful, the team must come back and execute again.

Let's say it's second down and ten yards to go. The quarterback throws a short pass over the middle. His eyes widen because it's almost intercepted. If it had been intercepted, the cornerback on the other team would have run for a touchdown. After the play, the quarterback is back in the huddle. What's he going to think? What's he going to do?

The quarterback has to do three things. (1) He must learn from his mistake of throwing the ball late. (2) He must decide what he is going to do on the next play. (3) He must recover from the mistake and move on to the next play! The more he plays, the less he will make that mistake again. What would happen if he said to himself, "I shouldn't have thrown that pass; it was almost intercepted. I guess I just shouldn't play football." Nonsense!

There are times when failure is a natural consequence of living. In fact, God often uses trials and failures as a learning process in our lives. When He does this, we learn, as Epps said, by doing. In James 1:2-4 the NIV Bible tells us, "Consider it pure joy, my brothers, when you face trials of many kinds, because you know that the testing of your faith develops perseverance. Perseverance must finish its work so that you may be mature and complete, not lacking anything."

Strategy and Tactics:

Through successful failure your son can learn and grow when he falls short. When he fails as a result of working hard to complete a worthwhile task, remind him he cannot lose—he can only make mistakes. Dr. Paul Brand, in his book, *Pain—the Gift Nobody Wants* reveals that pain experienced from failure and other sources enables us to grow and learn. Your son needs to understand that, at times, he will need to embrace the successful failures he experiences so that he will grow as a result of those failures. But he also needs to learn that he can recover from unsuccessful failure too.

There are times, however, when we fail because we run from responsibility. Sometimes we run because we aren't prepared for the challenge we face. Sometimes we run because we fear the criticism we might receive from our peers as a result of taking the responsibility. And sometimes we run because we fear the possibility of failure.

Fail, Forgive, and Fortify

Failure can have another name—sin. Sin, simply put, is falling short of God's perfect standard, which results in broken fellowship with Him. Whether we sin by active disobedience or rebellion, or by passive indifference, the result is the same. But we can recover from this type of failure and make it successful.

When we avoid responsibility, we must get back into the game as soon as possible. The recovery progresses in three stages:

I. **Fail:** We make the wrong decision, do the wrong thing, or find ourselves unable to succeed in a task.

II. **Forgive:** If sin is involved, we seek to restore fellowship with God by asking His forgiveness for our mistake. Then we forgive ourselves for our poor choice and weakness. We also seek forgiveness from people we have hurt.

III. **Fortify:** We recognize God's forgiveness for our failure and His grace for our limitations, learn from our mistakes, and try again.

The Bible describes how the apostle Peter recovered after failing Jesus several times.

1. Check out Matthew 16:21-23. How did Peter respond toward Jesus and his prediction of his own suffering and death? How did Jesus respond to Peter?

    Answer: Peter rebuked Jesus and insisted that Jesus would not be killed. Then Jesus scolded Peter, referred to him as Satan, and told him he was a stumbling block to the work of God.

2. According to Luke 22:54-62, what did Peter do when Jesus was on the verge of being crucified?

    Answer: Peter denied three times that he knew Jesus or was one of his disciples.

3. What do you think Peter's responsibility was to Jesus in this situation?

    Answer: Peter could have stood up and acknowledged his connection with Jesus, he could have encouraged Jesus in this difficult time, and he could have spoken to the chief priest on Jesus' behalf.

4. Why do you think Peter ran from responsibility and failed Jesus in His time of need?

    Answer: He let fear control him and abandoned Jesus. He did not trust Christ to do what He promised because the circumstances did not seem to be going in his favor.

5. Read John 21:15-19 and Acts 2:38-47. Was Peter able to recover from his failures to obey and follow Christ? How do you know?

    Answer: Jesus forgave Peter for denying him and then encouraged him to continue his mission of teaching and caring for others. Peter went on to lead many people to faith in Christ and was a key leader in the rapid growth of the early church.

Question #1 Tip:

Ask your son: How would you feel about being "chewed out" by Jesus face-to-face?

✦ Session 4 ✦

QUESTION #6 TIP:

The early teen years are a particularly rough time for boys to feel good about themselves. Be sensitive and encouraging for your son. Encourage him that you believe in his ability to recover from a failure.

Even though large tracts of Europe have fallen or may fall into the grip of the Gestapo and all the odious apparatus of Nazi rule, we shall not flag nor fail. We shall go on to the end, we shall fight in France, we shall fight on the seas and the oceans, we shall fight with growing confidence and growing strength in the air, we shall defend our island, whatever the cost may be ... we shall never surrender.

Winston Churchill (before Parliament in June 1940)

Peter was one of Jesus' closest friends. In fact, Jesus referred to Peter as the "Rock" because of his faith and strength of character. When Jesus told Peter that all of His friends would eventually deny him, Peter promised that he would never do such a thing. And yet, Peter ran from his responsibility on the night Jesus was crucified. When asked about his friendship with Christ, Peter denied that he even knew Jesus three times!

"What a cowardly failure Peter was!" we might say. How could he recover from such a mistake? He not only sought forgiveness from God for his mistake, but he went on to become one of the most powerful preachers the world has ever known. Peter recovered!

6. Have you ever felt like a failure the way Teknon felt after the battle? Do you think God understands that you aren't perfect?

7. Read Psalm 103:13-14 and 1 Corinthians 1:25-27. What do these verses teach us about our own strength and God's understanding of how we're put together?

   Answer: God created us so He knows our weaknesses and failures. And yet, God still has compassion on us as a loving father would. Our awesome God loves you in all your weakness and wants to use you to help build His kingdom and bring glory to His name!

God knows that we make mistakes. He knows us better than we know ourselves because He created us. If you've made a mistake, you can recover. If you've run from responsibility, you can recover. If you've been criticized, you can recover. God has unlimited power to enable you to recover, recover, and recover again. Remember, successful failure is not a bad thing. But if your failure is a sin, you must admit your failure to God, choose not to make the bad choice again, and return to walking with God. If you do these things, He promises to restore you.

8. As a result of what you've learned in this session, how will you handle successful and unsuccessful failures differently in the future? Do you think that Teknon will learn how to recover and get back into the battle?

Press on to episode 9 of the story.

> The Main Thing I Learned from Episode 8:
>
> _____
>
> _____
>
> _____
>
> _____

Important Note:

Remind your son that if he has invited Jesus Christ into his life, he has access to God's forgiveness for his unsuccessful failures. When he sins, he should confess it to God, turn away from that attitude or behavior (repent), and recover by moving on with the assurance that God has forgiven him. Confession and repentance will immediately restore his fellowship with God.

Main Things:

If needed, help your son by suggesting some key truths that he should have learned during this session. For example, ask your son to discuss the difference between successful and unsuccessful failure and how to deal with each type. Or, you might highlight the importance of facing fears and of learning how to recover.

Session 5: Episodes 9 and 10 of Teknon and the Champion Warriors

Episode 9: Recover, Recover, Recover

Champion Characteristics

Courage and Mental Toughness

Power Verse: Psalm 56:3-4

When I am afraid, I will put my trust in You. In God, whose word I praise, in God I have put my trust; I shall not be afraid. What can mere man do to me?

Story Summary

Teknon's apprehension spills over into episode 9 as he realizes that he must act to save his father and friends. Matty gives Teknon a crash course in leadership, coaching him in how to enlist the aid of other people. Teknon hesitates because he does not want to enter a situation where he may not be accepted. But, Teknon realizes the magnitude of the situation and is forced to break out of his comfort zone. He runs to get help in the nearby mining village.

Help comes in the form of a stocky little fellow named Phileo. Phileo belongs to a race known as the Phaskos. Even though Teknon is barraged with negative messages transmitted from Scandalon on his way to the

Episode 9 Overview:

In this session, you and your son will explore what it means to live courageously—facing fears, getting out of comfort zones, and standing for what is right. You will also discuss the importance of seeking respect from other people rather than doing things for their acceptance. Finally, you will discuss the potential paralysis of discouragement, as well as the importance of recovering from failure. Session 5 will delve deeper into the topic of managing discouragement.

Phasko village, the urgency of the situation helps him overcome his lack of confidence and his inhibitions. He convinces Phileo and the other Phaskos to help him. On their return trip to where the team is entrapped, Teknon comes face to face with Scandalon, who inflicts a gash on Teknon's arm before Phileo comes to his aid.

After the rescue is complete, his team members congratulate Teknon for his courage in overcoming his fears and in gaining the help they needed. Then Kratos and Phileo, nicknamed Phil, acknowledge a long-term friendship. Phil is the informant they've been seeking.

Discussion Topics

Break out of your "comfort zone"

Be respected vs. liked

Recovering from failure — part 2: don't give in to discouragement

Reconnaissance

1. Recite the CHAMPION Warrior Creed out loud. Pause before you say the lines about courage and mental toughness.

2. Review the Map of the Mission on page 8 to determine the team's location in episode 9.

3. Review the CHAMPION definitions of **Courage** and **Mental Toughness** (refer to the CHAMPION Code on page 6).

    Answer for Courage: "I will cultivate bravery and trust in God. I will break out of my comfort zone by seeking to conquer my fears. I will learn to recover, recover, and recover again."

Answer for Mental Toughness: "I will allow God to direct my thinking toward gaining common sense and wisdom. I will use discernment when making hard decisions. I will desire respect from others rather than compromise my convictions for acceptance or approval

4. Why did Teknon hesitate to go to the village? What was he afraid of?

    Answer: He was afraid to confront people. He was also afraid of the rejection he might experience from those people after presenting his plea for help.

5. Why did Tor tell Teknon not to worry about being liked by the Phaskos? What did Tor say about respect? What did he mean?

    Answer: Tor told Teknon that the only thing that matters is that the Phaskos respect his position. He essentially told him that it was far more important to be respected than to be liked.

6. Look back at episode 4 where Teknon meets the Harpax. Why do you think acceptance by the Harpax was so important to Teknon?

    Answer: Teknon's desire for acceptance is the same as it is for most teenagers— he wants to fit in and be a part of the group. He wants others to be recognized and viewed as a worthwhile person by his peers.

7. What did Scandalon do to Teknon on his way to the village? Why?

    Answer: Scandalon tried to deceive and discourage Teknon in order to dissolve his confidence and keep him from accomplishing his objective.

In the world you have tribulation, but take courage; I [Jesus] have overcome the world.

John 16:33b

✦ Session 5 ✦

QUESTION #9 TIP:

Sometimes we need to remember the battle scars, emotional and spiritual, that we have received during difficult times in our lives. These scars have helped us to grow as men. Share with your son about a time when God led you through a difficult experience and what you learned from it.

Be on the alert, stand firm in the faith, act like men, be strong.

1 Corinthians 16:13

BREAK OUT TIP:

To a young man it's not just the task of accomplishing something he fears that concerns him. He probably also struggles with the desire to be accepted and liked. In this section you will also have the opportunity to explore with your son how to deal with his longing to be liked and accepted by his peers.

8. Why did Teknon respond differently to Scandalon's voice on the way back to the clearing?

   Answer: With renewed confidence, Teknon listened more closely; once he identified the source of the voice, his insecurity faded and he changed his focus.

9. Why did Teknon want to keep the scar on his arm?

   Answer: Teknon kept the scar as a reminder of the lessons he learned during the experience of rescuing his father and mentors. Tor described it as a badge of courage because Teknon faced his fear and conquered it.

10. Do you think Teknon recovered from his failure in episode 8? If so, how?

    Answer: Teknon moved beyond his failure and refocused his efforts on his objective instead of on himself and his failure. With a renewed focus, he proceeded to the Phasko village where he succeeded in his objective to get help. He recovered!

STRATEGY AND TACTICS

BREAK OUT OF THE ZONE!

Have you ever heard an athlete say, "I was in the zone"? For an athlete, being "in the zone" refers to playing a sport far beyond what he considers his normal ability. If you've had that experience, you know how good it feels to experience that kind of performance. There's another zone, however, that also feels good, but for another reason. It's called the "comfort zone."

You feel good in your comfort zone because life feels easy. The comfort zone is a place where you do things because it's the way you've always done them.

1. Have you ever been afraid to take on a particularly difficult task, or work closely with someone who really seems not to like you, or ask for the help from someone who you're afraid to approach?

   We break out of our comfort zone by facing our fears. When we face and conquer fears with God's help, we experience personal, emotional, and spiritual victory.

God Provides the Power to Break Out of the Zone

2. What does King David tell you about who God is and what He does for you in Psalm 27:1,13-14?

   Answer: God is his light (dispelling anxieties and dangers), his salvation (guaranteed victory), and his defense (stronghold against any assaults). With God on his side, David says he has nothing or nobody to fear. Verse 13 highlights that God is good. He is always looking out for your son's good, no matter how things may seem.

   Every noble work is at first impossible.

   Thomas Carlyle

3. What does Psalm 27:1,13-14 tell you not to do? What does it tell you that you should do?

   Answer: DO NOT fear or dread things or people. DO NOT despair because God is good. DO believe in God's goodness. DO wait for the Lord and His direction and timing of events. DO be strong and let your heart take courage.

Breaking Out of the Zone Is Profitable but Not Always Popular

Often, our biggest barrier to break out of our comfort zone is our own fear of what others might say. Nobody likes to be criticized, and nobody likes to be misunderstood. When we do something outside our comfort zone, like giving a speech or sharing our faith in God with someone else, we put our egos at risk. Let's face it: we like to be liked. But it's not necessary to be liked by everyone. At times, people are going to misunderstand us. At other times, people will also become angry with us even when we do the right thing!

4. Read Psalm 56:3-4. If you trust in God, what can others do to you?

    Answer: The psalmist asks, "What can mere man do to me?" The answer is obvious: nothing! The real question is, do we really believe this? In Romans 8:31b Paul asks, "If God is for us, who is against us?" Our God is awesome in His power.

5. What does Jesus warn us about living in this world in John 15:15-16? How should we expect to be liked and accepted if we are His friends and follow Him?

    Answer: Jesus said we shouldn't be surprised if the world hates us (His followers and friends), because it hated Him first. We must expect that people in this world will not always accept us if we choose to follow God.

6. What does 2 Timothy 1:7 say about fear?

    Answer: God did not create us to be fearful and timid about carrying out the tasks He gives us, but rather

---

We all are faced with a series of great opportunities brilliantly disguised as impossible situations.

Charles Swindoll

QUOTE TIP:

Ask your son what this quote means. Then, give your son an example from your life when you faced what appeared to be an impossible situation, but God worked through it and turned it into a great opportunity.

to draw on His power to live courageously by faith. We also need to draw on His love and seek a sound mind to focus on His truth instead of the lies of the devil.

7. What does Jesus say about the truth (God's Word) in John 8:32?

   Answer: Jesus tells us that we should abide in His Word and learn the truth. Knowing and living by the real truth revealed in God's Word will set us free from sin and the lies of the devil. When you hear false voices, replace them with the truth of God's Word. If you have invited Christ into your life by faith, you are a child of the King. Neither people nor Satan's messengers can intimidate you unless you let them.

According to Henry Blackaby and Claude King, authors of *Experiencing God*, God is working all around us. When we seek to develop our personal relationship with Him, which began when we invited Him into our lives by faith, He provides opportunities to join Him where He is working. These invitations usually take us out of our comfort zone. But if we step outside the zone (and allow God to accomplish what only He can), we grow as individuals as well as in our relationship with Him.

Everybody ought to do at least two things each day that he hates to do, just for practice.

Will James

Breaking Out of the Zone Is Worth the Risk

At times, God asks us to step out of our comfort zone to obey His will. We may not know how we are going to accomplish it, but we know that He wants it done. That's when God expects us to trust in Him by faith and watch Him bring about the results.

8. Read Matthew 17:20. If we have faith in God, what does He say that we can do? How much faith do we need in order to see God do mighty things?

◆ Session 5 ◆

Main Things:

If needed, help your son by suggesting some key truths that he should have learned during this session, such as the importance of breaking out of his comfort zone when God leads him to new opportunities and challenges. You may want to remind him of the three important factors for breaking out of comfort zones: (1) God provides the power to break out of the zone, (2) breaking out of the zone is profitable but not always popular, and (3) breaking out of the zone is worth the risk.

You gain strength, courage, and confidence by every experience in which you really stop to look fear in the face ... You must do the thing you think you cannot do.

Eleanor Roosevelt

Answer: If you have faith as small as a tiny mustard seed, God can even move a mountain. Without faith, it is impossible to please God, but with a little faith nothing is impossible if God wants to do it for you.

9. Name three things that would take you out of your comfort zone.

   (1)

   (2)

   (3)

The Main Thing I Learned from Episode 9:

_____

_____

_____

_____

_____

Episode 10: Good Enough

CHAMPION Characteristics

Attitude and Integrity

Power Verse: 1 Corinthians 9:24–25a

Do you not know that those who run in a race all run, but only one receives the prize? Run in such a way that you may win. Everyone who competes in the games exercises self-control in all things.

Story Summary

Phil joins the warriors as they travel to the Northron Peninsula. "Passive" is the best word to describe the people and lifestyle of this tropical paradise. Unfortunately, Northrons have abandoned all desire to rise above a life of leisure. They have settled into a mindset of mediocrity; characterized by their oft-spoken motto: "good enough." Because Northrons refuse to improve themselves and their surroundings, they have neglected the vital foundations of their lives.

The team uses Northros as a temporary base before entering the mountains to challenge Magos in his fortress. Kratos and Matty leave their companions to perform reconnaissance of enemy territory, while the other team members stay in Northros. During their stay, the warriors engage in a fierce battle with a creature called a Leviathan. This confrontation is a result of the apathetic negligence of the Northrons. In the battle, the team saves a young woman named Paranomia. During the struggle, one of the Northron men abandons the young woman during the struggle. Tor, greatly frustrated by the Northron's attitudes and lifestyle, unleashes his temper by throwing and injuring the young man, whom

✦ Session 5 ✦

Epps later heals. Afterward, Tor's conscience gets the best of him and he asks forgiveness from the young man.

Discussion Topics

Pursue excellence

Resist mediocrity

Manage your anger

Reconnaissance

1. Recite the CHAMPION Warrior Creed together from memory (see page 5).

2. Review the Map of the Mission on page 8 to determine the team's location in episode 10.

3. Review the CHAMPION definition of **Integrity**.

    Answer: "I will seek to acquire a clear understanding of who I am in Christ so that I may have a deeper comprehension of what I believe, what I stand for, and how I can live out those convictions in the most difficult circumstances, whether I am alone or with others. I will allow other people to hold me accountable to standards of excellence."

4. Phil said that the Northrons enjoyed mediocrity. How is this revealed in their lives?

    Answer: Through their actions and speech. Northrons showed no motivation to improve themselves or their environment. They also showed no interest to help each other.

5. Tor said that the Northrons "have no vision ... no purpose ... no plan." He said, "Where there's no purpose, there's no passion for living." Why is it important to have vision, purpose, and a plan in our lives?

   Answer: Over time, God, through our relationship with Him, gives us the vision He has for our lives. From this vision we gain the full, meaningful passion for living that only He can provide. From this passion, we have a sustained, productive, and exciting purpose in everything we do. Personal integrity involves taking the responsibility to pursue excellence and exercise discipline in every area of our lives so that God can accomplish His exciting purpose through us.

6. Why did Tor lose his temper?

   Answer: Tor was angered because of the Northrons' lack of initiative, especially when it concerned helping each other. Tor was especially angered by the young man's cowardly response to saving the young girl from the leviathan.

7. Do you think that Tor had a right to get angry? Why or why not? Was it okay for him to hurt the Northron?

   Answer: The Bible tells us we can be angry for the right reasons, but we still should not sin (see Ephesians 4:26). Tor sinned when he lost control of his emotions and hurt the Northron.

8. How did Tor feel after he lost his temper? What did he do after he hurt the Northron? Why?

   Answer: He felt guilty because he recognized his lack of self-control. After he regained his composure, Tor went back to the Northron and asked his forgiveness for the attack. The CHAMPION Warrior Code states: "I will improve my ability to manage anger." Tor knew that the teachings of Pneuma included the principle of managing anger effectively.

> *Hold yourself responsible to a higher standard than anyone else expects of you. Never excuse yourself.*
>
> Henry Ward Beecher

✦ Session 5 ✦

> *The best preparation for tomorrow is doing your best today.*
>
> H. Jackson Brown, Jr.

9. What did Epps say was a sign of true strength in Tor? What did Epps mean by that?

Answer: The sign of true strength was Tor's willingness to humbly ask for forgiveness. Epps meant that it takes strength of character to humble yourself, admit that you are wrong, and ask another person for forgiveness.

> *Let us run with endurance the race that is set before us.*
>
> Hebrews 12:1b

Strategy and Tactics

Lukewarm is Not Good Enough

1. Revelation 3:15-16 describes the church at Laodicea. What kind of attitude is Jesus describing here? And what is His response toward this type of attitude?

Answer: Jesus says their deeds are neither cold nor hot. Jesus is describing the attitude of being lukewarm or indifferent to God's principles, compromising, accommodating, and "on the fence." This is the attitude that says, "I don't care; it's good enough." This attitude is so disgusting to the Lord and so damaging to His purposes that He says it makes Him feel sick!

2. According to Ephesians 5:15-17, how should we use our time?

   Answer: The NIV translates this as follows: "Be very careful, then, how you live—not as unwise but as wise, making the most of every opportunity, because the days are evil. Therefore, do not be foolish, but understand what the Lord's will is." We need to be wise and careful in how we live. We must live our lives with God's vision, purpose, and plan for our lives.

3. What do you think it means to "make the most of every opportunity"?

   Answer: We must always be ready (training) and available (attitude) to be used by God whenever He provides an opportunity.

4. Read Luke 2:40-52. In what ways was Jesus growing as a person even though He was only 12 years old?

   Answer: Verse 52 says, "And Jesus kept increasing in wisdom and stature, and in favor with God and men." He was assuming greater levels of responsibility in His life. He was growing mentally (wisdom), physically (stature), spiritually (favor with God), and socially (favor with men).

God expects us to be thankful for the talents and opportunities He gives us. He also expects us to make the most of the life and gifts He has provided. The story in Luke 2 declares that Jesus grew and kept increasing in stature (physically), in wisdom (mentally), in favor with men (socially), and in favor with God (spiritually). Jesus was a good steward of what God the Father had entrusted to Him. He set an example for us to keep increasing in our maturity by avoiding mediocrity in our lives.

Average is your enemy.

Pearce "Rocky" Lane

QUOTE TIP:

Ask your son, "What does this quotation mean? Why would 'average' be your enemy? How do you fight this enemy?"

If you accept "average" you will never rise above mediocrity. You fight average by continually challenging yourself. You can't lower your standards to meet those around us.

♦ SESSION 5 ♦

5. In Matthew 19:26 what does Jesus say is possible with God?

   Answer: Although Jesus is talking here about salvation and entering heaven, He also points out that this (and many other things) is impossible for men, but ALL THINGS are possible with God.

6. Read Philippians 4:13. If we are Christians, what can we do as a result of God's power working through us?

   Answer: "I can do all things through Him [the Lord] who strengthens me."

Use Your Head; Don't Lose Your Head!

> *Speak when you're angry, and you'll make the best speech you'll ever regret.*
>
> Anonymous

Do you have a short fuse? When people disagree with you or fail to meet your expectations does your response look something like the fireworks at Walt Disney World? How often do you lose your patience or "blow up" with other people?

It's almost fashionable to have a short fuse, isn't it? Even violent anger is recognized as the status quo.

7. How do you think a person learns to manage anger?

   Answer: We learn by deepening our relationship with God, living according to His principles, and following Christ's example so that we become "conformed to the image of Christ" (Romans 8:29-30). Then, we draw on His strength to control our emotions.

The Bible talks about the process of managing anger as a key component of self-control. Self-control is one of the outward expressions of Christ's presence in our lives as we learn to entrust our lives to Him. The Bible calls these characteristics the "fruit of the Spirit."

8. Read Galatians 5:22-23. What is the fruit of the Spirit?

   Answer: The fruit of the Spirit is a collection of nine characteristics produced by the Spirit in those who walk in dependence on Him (see verse 5:16). The collection is: love, joy, peace, patience, kindness, goodness, faithfulness, gentleness, and self-control.

Uncontrolled anger, like so many other things, can become a habit. Once you get used to "losing your head", it becomes easier to let it happen the next time. Tor developed a habit of losing his temper until he decided to become a CHAMPION Warrior. He knew that self-control was a key characteristic of a CHAMPION and didn't want to accept "good enough" in his life.

If you are a Christian, God expects you to overcome a bad temper by drawing on His power. We plug into His strength by being filled with His Spirit. When you are filled with the Holy Spirit, you start displaying the fruit of the Spirit. It is one thing to hate evil and become angered by its presence in the world. It's another thing to take out frustrations on others. When we do that, we disobey God. If you sense that you have disobeyed God through a fit of bad temper, remember 1 John 1:9 and confess your anger to Him. He will forgive you and reestablish His line of communication and power with you.

But we could spend our lives trying to manage anger after it has erupted. How do we keep from losing our temper ahead of time? The book of James describes an effective formula for anger prevention.

9. Read James 1:19-20. What three things should we do to keep from losing our temper?

Answer:

God's Power + _____Quick to Hear or Listen_____ + _____Slow to Speak_____ + _____Slow to Anger_____
= Anger Management

Keeping our mouths shut is one of the hardest things in the world to do when we get upset. It's also one of the most effective tools in anger management. A spoken word is like a football right before it's intercepted. As much as the quarterback wants it back, he can't get it back. If there is any question whether or not you should say something, DON'T SAY IT!

Instead of being quick to speak, use the other highly effective tool in anger management. Learn to listen. Author Stephen Covey says, "Seek first to understand, then to be understood." Listen not only to what's being said, but also to what isn't being said. Try to put yourself in the other person's shoes so you can better understand his or her position. God knows that you get angry; He created anger to alert you that something is wrong. But when you get angry, draw on His strength to remain calm and under the control of His Spirit. Use your head; don't lose your head!

> *Don't fly into a rage unless you are prepared for a rough landing.*
>
> Anonymous

The Main Thing I Learned from Episode 10:

_____
_____
_____
_____
_____

Main Things:

If needed, help your son by suggesting some key truths that he should have learned during this session, such as the importance of pursuing excellence rather than settling for "good enough" in different areas of his life, and the formula for anger management.

Session 6: Episodes 11 and 12 of Teknon and the CHAMPION Warriors

Episode 11: The Element of Doubt

CHAMPION Characteristics

Integrity and Purity

Power Verse: 1 Thessalonians 5:21-22

But examine everything carefully; hold fast to that which is good; abstain from every form of evil.

Story summary

Magos takes full advantage of Kratos' absence from the rest of the team in episode 11. The cyborg speaks to Teknon through a holographic image and confuses Teknon about his belief in the CHAMPION principles and way of life. Teknon becomes mentally and emotionally vulnerable. As he grapples with his own uncertainty, he seeks a temporary diversion to relieve his frustration and stress.

He finds his escape in the company of Pary, the young woman rescued by the team in episode 10. Teknon spends the better part of three days with Pary enjoying activities around the Northron Peninsula. While Teknon views his time with Pary as fun and diverting, Pary interprets his interest in her as more than platonic.

Episode 11 Overview:

Does your son know who he is as a Christian and what he stands for? Does he have strong assurance of his position in Christ and an understanding of personal integrity?

In this episode, you and your son will have the opportunity to discuss the importance of maintaining personal convictions and understanding the emotional side of relationships—particularly between a young man and young woman. Although Teknon does not engage in a physically sexual relationship with Pary, except to hold her hand, he still carelessly manipulates her emotions and treats her insensitively. He uses her to meet his needs for relaxation and to hide from his inner doubts and confusion, while leading her on emotionally. Take this opportunity during your son's CHAMPION training to start preparing him for the inevitable challenges to his faith that he will face as he grows.

Epps warns Teknon about miscommunicating his intentions to Pary. Teknon is surprised and alarmed when Pary discloses her feelings for him. At first, Teknon is overcome with embarrassment as Pary storms off deeply hurt. Then, Teknon experiences regret as he realizes the effect of his insensitivity to Pary.

The episode ends with the return of Kratos and Matty from their reconnaissance of Mago's fortress.

Discussion Topics

Know who I am

Identify my personal convictions

Live out my convictions

Avoid romantic relationships and entanglements too early

Reconnaissance

1. Recite the CHAMPION Warrior Creed from memory. If you can, invite two or more people to be in the room when you say it.

2. Review the Map of the Mission on page 8 before beginning this section. Identify where the team is located in episode 11.

3. Review the CHAMPION definitions of **Integrity** and **Purity** (refer to the CHAMPION Code on page 6).

   Answer for Integrity: "I will seek to acquire a clear understanding of who I am in Christ so that I may have a deeper comprehension of what I believe, what I stand for, and how I can live out those convictions in the most difficult circumstances, whether I am alone or with others. I will allow other people to hold me accountable to standards of excellence."

Answer for Purity: "I will train myself to keep the temple of my body and mind uncorrupted mentally, emotionally, and physically. I will commit to avoid and flee sexual temptation."

4. How did Magos try to confuse Teknon?

   Answer: Magos tried to convince him that Kratos had lied. Magos also implied that the mission to retrieve the Logos was misguided.

5. Why do you think Magos challenged Teknon about his beliefs? What did Epps have to say about this?

   Answer: (Epps speaking): "Magos wanted to create doubt in your mind about your beliefs so that you would feel frightened and insecure. He knows that you're young in your convictions, and he wants to take advantage of that. ... Magos knows that if he can confuse and tempt you, your father will become concerned ... distracted, and more open to attack."

   Magos wanted to place the element of doubt into Teknon's mind about his convictions and mission. He used this tactic to try to turn Teknon to his way to thinking as well as to distract Kratos and make him more vulnerable to attack.

> *Magos wanted to create doubt in your mind about your beliefs, so that you would feel frightened and insecure.*
>
> Epps

◆ SESSION 6 ◆

Failure to prepare is preparing to fail.

John Wooden

An expert at anything was once a beginner.

H. Jackson Browne

6. Why did Teknon enjoy spending time with Pary?

   Answer: Because Pary offered Teknon an enjoyable escape from the pressure and stress he was experiencing on the mission.

7. Describe how Teknon treated Pary during the three days they spent together.

   Answer: Teknon was friendly, but he also led Pary to believe that he cared for her romantically. He used her to meet his needs for relaxation, to have a fun time with a young woman his age, and to mentally escape from his inner doubts and confusion.

8. After his conversation with Epps, what did Teknon realize that he had done wrong?

   Answer: He realized that he had communicated incorrect intentions to Pary. Instead of treating her like a friend, he had carelessly encouraged her to have an emotional attachment to him.

9. How did Pary respond when Teknon talked with her that last morning on the beach? Why did she react this way?

   Answer: She was surprised and hurt. She reacted angrily because she thought Teknon felt the same way that she did. Teknon's miscommunication through his words and actions reinforced her distrust of people, which was based upon her previous experiences with the Northrons.

10. How could Teknon have prevented this from happening and still maintained his friendship with Pary?

    Answer: He could have been more careful in his speech. He also could have refrained from physical contact. It would have been wise for him to include other people in their daily trips so that the two were not alone for extended periods of time.

Strategy and Tactics

1. Read Luke 4:1-13. Who was challenged? – and by whom?

    Answer: Jesus was tempted and challenged by the devil himself.

2. How did Jesus respond to the temptations and challenges made to Him?

Verses to consider	Temptation / Challenge	Jesus' response
Luke 4:3-4	Are you the Son of God? Prove it by turning this stone into bread!	He quoted from the Bible (Deuteronomy 8:3) that man does not live on bread alone.
Luke 4:5-8	Just worship me, and I'll give you all the kingdoms of this earthly world.	He quoted from the Bible (Deuteronomy 6:13) that you are to worship and serve only the Lord.
Luke 4:9-12	Are you the Son of God? If so, jump off from here. God promises to use angels to care for you, so you won't get hurt.	He quoted from the Bible (Deuteronomy 6:16) that you should not put the Lord your God to the test.

Important Note

Does your son have strong assurance of his position in Christ and an understanding of personal integrity? These are big questions for a young man. But the sooner he starts thinking through the details of his values and convictions, the less likely he will be to stray from those tracks during the years ahead. We live in a cynical world, one in which skeptics enjoy any opportunity to challenge the claims of a committed Christian with the element of doubt. Ultimately, of course, your own personal example, as his dad, will provide the greatest evidence to your son that you have a personal relationship with Jesus Christ.

But challenges will come. And when they do, we, as Christians, should be prepared to provide a response. It is important, therefore, to know what we believe and why we believe it. You can help your son clarify many potential issues. During the coming years your son may be challenged on such issues as:

His assurance of salvation. "How can you know that you're going to heaven?" a skeptic might ask. Help your son realize that he can know with certainty that he has a future residence in heaven.

The attributes of God. "How can you believe in one God, who is all-powerful, all-knowing, perfectly just, and merciful?" is another common question. God's attributes are unchanging, indicative of who He is.

His actions in accordance with God's plan for his life. "How can you believe that you should live your life according to the teachings of a bunch of men, written down thousands of years ago? What makes you think that you can know God's will?" How would your

Jesus was very tired and hungry when Satan challenged His beliefs. But instead of becoming unsettled when Satan tried to use the element of doubt, Jesus quoted Scripture to strengthen his position. He confidently relied on the words of His Heavenly Father.

If you have accepted Jesus as your personal Savior by faith, sooner or later you will get challenged about why you believe in Jesus. If that happens, great! You will have the opportunity to go back to the Bible to find the answers to the challenges given to you. By doing that, you will fuel your confidence and reinforce your position in Christ! If you need help, ask your parents, your pastor, or someone else whom you respect to point you to Bible verses and other Bible-based materials that apply to your situation.

Better yet, even when someone else is not challenging you, spend time reading and studying the Bible now so that you will become more knowledgeable about what it means to be a Christian and apply God's truth each day.

3. Most everyone has asked himself or herself, "What will my friends think if I stand up for what I believe?" Why is that such an important question to us?

Answer: It can seem easier to do whatever it takes to be liked and accepted by our peers, while it seems quite difficult to obey God and to do what people in authority over us (including our parents) tell us to do.

Build your character based on what God's Word has to say about His character. Don't get rattled like Teknon. He got stressed out over Magos' challenge, decided to take a break from reality in order to make himself feel better, and hurt himself and Pary in the process ... which leads us to our second topic.

What Does God Have to Say About Relationships?

"Learn to love appropriately. You need to use your head and test your feelings so that your love is sincere and intelligent, not sentimental gush." Philippians 1:9-10 (The Message)

4. It's nice when a girl shows you affection, isn't it? What could be more pleasant than when she calls you on the phone and tells you how great you are? It makes you feel like a million bucks, right? But when you feel that way, whose needs are you meeting—yours or hers? Are you giving in to "sentimental gush"?

   Answer: Flattery, especially from a young woman, is like soothing balm on a wound for a young man. If your son is not careful, he can let his motivations become self-centered. When that happens, the Bible says he's loving inappropriately.

   Emotions can be weird. When emotions get involved in a relationship between a young man and a young woman, friends start to become more than friends. At that point people often get hurt.

5. Read 1 Timothy 5:1-2. How are you supposed to treat young women if you will honor them and honor God?

   Answer: God's Word instructs us to treat older women as mothers, but to treat younger women as sisters. The verse adds the emphasis "in all purity" just to make sure we get the point.

6. Is it wise for me to be anything other than a friend to what the Bible calls my sisters in the Lord? Why or why not?

   Answer: In the illustration of the Shocktech during episode 3, Kratos explained to Teknon that "error increases with distance." If he allows himself to become romantically

son answer questions like this?

Take this opportunity, during your son's CHAMPION Training, to prepare him for the inevitable challenges to his faith that he will face throughout his teen and early adult years.

Reject passivity, accept responsibility, lead courageously, and expect God's reward.

Robert Lewis

Question #6 Tip:

Challenge your son to set some boundaries in the area of romantic relationships. Help him with ideas and help keep him accountable.

> *The gem cannot be polished without friction, nor man perfected without scars.*
>
> Chinese Proverb

involved with a young woman, even a Christian young woman, at this stage of his life, then where will he let his emotions take him in his late teens and early 20s? Making a decision to avoid teenage boyfriend-girlfriend relationships is obviously counter-cultural, but it is worth the investment. When, and if, the time comes for God to bring him a wife, she will be just the right person and will meet him in just the right context. Once they are married, they can share with integrity all the emotion and romance he and she have to offer.

The pressure to start dating and to begin relationships is happening progressively earlier in life. Don't allow yourself to start something romantic that you can't and shouldn't finish. Instead, seek to treat young women as cherished sisters, friends whom you can encourage. Don't get caught up in the gush because there is so much more to enjoy at this point by being friends. This delayed gratification (waiting for what I want until God gives it to me at the right time) will become tougher as the years go by, but God will bless you for making the right decisions. And your effort will be greatly rewarded — beyond whatever you could ask or think! God promises this in Ephesians 3:20. Check it out.

The Main Thing I Learned from Episode 11:

_____

_____

_____

_____

_____

Main Things:

If needed, help your son by suggesting some key truths that he should have learned during this session, such as the importance of avoiding romantic relationships with young women until the appropriate time (when he is older and ready for marriage), or the importance of studying God's Word to establish and defend his own beliefs.

✦ Session 6 ✦

Episode 12: Nothing More, Nothing Less, Nothing Else

Champion Characteristic

Attitude

Power Verse: 1 Corinthians 15:57-58

But thanks be to God, who gives us the victory through our Lord Jesus Christ. Therefore, my beloved brethren, be steadfast, immovable, always abounding in the work of the Lord, knowing that your toil is not in vain in the Lord.

Story Summary

The episode begins as the team splits into two groups when they reach the Thumos Mountains. Teknon, Phil, and Kratos begin to set up camp; the others scout out the trails ahead. A huge Seismos enters the campsite, eats the team's food, and moves to attack Teknon and Kratos. Phil uses his unique drilling skills to create a hole to capture the beast. The three salvage what gear they can and move to a different clearing. Phil digs a cave complete with stone beds, chairs, and a table. As the three settle in for the night, Kratos and Phil pray for the return of the other team members. Teknon's attitude worsens as he becomes discouraged, and frustrated with his circumstances.

At the end of episode 12, Teknon wakes from a sound sleep to a very dangerous predicament. He survived a traumatic battle the night before due to the heroic efforts of Kratos and Phil. He still hasn't emotionally recovered from the failure he had a few days ago. He awakens fatigued, famished, and frightened. He also realizes that he's alone! It appears that Phil and Kratos have been injured or worse. Alone, hungry, confused, tired—and ready to give up—Teknon finds the Hoplon in the snow.

DISCUSSION TOPICS:

Manage discouragement

Keep circumstances in proper perspective

Draw on God's strength and wisdom

RECONNAISSANCE

1. Recite the CHAMPION Warrior Creed from memory.

2. Review the Map of the Mission on page 8 and determine the team's location in episode 12.

3. Review the CHAMPION definition of **Attitude** (refer to the CHAMPION Code on page 6).

   Answer: "I will cultivate a disposition of humility. I will assume a correct and hopeful view of myself as a member of God's family. I will improve my ability to manage anger and discouragement. I will develop and enjoy an appropriate sense of humor."

EPISODE 12 OVERVIEW:

This episode focuses on how to manage discouragement. During the next few years, your son will have the dubious pleasure of heading into an uncharted territory known as young adulthood. While piloting his way through peer pressure, relationships with young women, school's challenges, and other rigors of daily life, he may be "shot down" in the enemy territory of discouragement. Your son's emotional health may be affected by many factors, including his family, friends, diet, sleep patterns, and, of course, his relationship with God. Discouragement can send him into a downward spiral.

◆ SESSION 6 ◆

4. What were some of the things that contributed to Teknon's discouragement?

   Answer:

   ▲ The way he mishandled his relationship with Pary.
   ▲ Allowing Magos to confuse him about the mission and his convictions.
   ▲ The difficulties and dangers he experienced during the mission.
   ▲ His fatigue and hunger after the encounter with the seismos.
   ▲ He was tired of making mistakes.

5. What, according to Kratos and Phil, is the way to overcome discouragement?

   Answer: They told Teknon to stay focused on completing the mission and to gain strength from Pneuma.

6. Phil told Teknon, "Even when our emotions tell us otherwise, we must stay focused on trusting Pneuma to help us make the right choices." Do you think our emotions are dependable? Why or why not?

   Answer: Our emotions are good indicators of problems, but they are not dependable. Developing the ability to control and deal with emotions, especially in the midst of discouragement, is a mark of maturity.

Victory belongs to the most persevering.

Napoleon

A real leader faces the music, even when he doesn't like the tune.

Unknown

Strategy and Tactics

Many things can cause us to feel discouraged and cause us to start going downhill emotionally. The more we get discouraged and lose hope, the farther down we go. Let's look at several categories of downhills that can cause discouragement.

Category 1: Health Downhills

- ▲ **Lack of sleep.** Former President Teddy Roosevelt said, "Fatigue makes cowards of us all." If we don't get enough sleep, we can become irritable and start to "cycle down."
- ▲ **Bad diet.** Too much sugar, caffeine, and fat can wreak havoc on our minds and our emotional stability.
- ▲ **Lack of exercise.** When we exercise, blood pumps oxygen into our blood and sends hormones called endorphins through our bodies to make us feel alert and energetic. When we spend too much time being a couch potato, we feel and act like sedated slugs.

Category 2: Head Downhills

- ▲ **Criticism from peers.** Overly critical people can have a negative effect on our attitudes and actions.
- ▲ **"Successful" failure.** We can become discouraged when we fail at doing the right things, like trying our best but still losing the game.
- ▲ **Stress.** Too much activity makes us feel like we're under the pile and unable to dig out.

Category 3: Heart Downhills

▲ **Unresolved conflict.** If we haven't reconnected with friends or family after an argument, we will experience a lack of closure until the problem is resolved.

▲ **"Unsuccessful" failure.** When we make a bad choice and disobey God (sin), we will feel miserable.

▲ **Unconfessed sin.** When we don't acknowledge to God that we have sinned and ask His forgiveness, guilt and discouragement will follow.

Teknon's discouragement related to all three of these categories. He was tired and hungry. He had unresolved conflict with Pary. Magos also confused him with criticism of the CHAMPION principles, which caused Teknon to doubt his beliefs and the team's mission. All of these circumstances prompted him to lose hope and start riding the downhill of discouragement.

Until you do what you believe in, you don't know whether you believe it or not.

Leo Tolstoy

1. How might Teknon have avoided becoming discouraged?

2. What kind of things get you down emotionally or spiritually?

3. Is there anything bothering you that you need to discuss? If so, what do you plan to do?

There's a lot you can do to dodge discouragement. To avoid the health downhills, you need to eat right, get enough sleep, and get on a regular exercise program. To avoid the head downhills, you should try not to spend too much time with negative people. You should also recover when you have an "unsuccessful" failure, and prioritize your time by involving yourself in only a few activities at a time.

As for avoiding the heart downhills, you should make sure that you are doing what you can to clear up unresolved arguments with others. Most importantly, you need to remember the importance of staying in communication with Jesus Christ. If you have unconfessed sin in your life, the phone lines are cut between you and God. You need to remember how to reconnect those communication lines through confession and turning away from your sin and toward God (repentance).

4. Remember 1 John 1:9? What does that verse say we need to do if we have disobeyed God?

    Answer: Confess our sin to Him.

5. What does God promise to do in return?

    Answer: God promises to forgive our sin and cleanse us from all unrighteousness.

The longer we ride the downhill of discouragement, the more we take our eyes off the One who can help us. Soon, we start losing hope and forgetting about the big picture. God doesn't want us to become discouraged.

6. You looked at Hebrews 12:1-2 in an earlier session. Look at it again, but this time focus on the first part of verse 2: "fixing our eyes on Jesus, the author and perfecter of faith ... " These verses talk about how we run the race of life that God has marked out for us and how we run to win. What is the big key to success that you find in verse 2?

    Answer: These verses plead with us to throw off everything that hinders, especially sin (through confession and repentance). Then the passage encourages us that we can run our race with endurance and hope IF we keep our eyes fixed on Jesus instead of on our problems.

✦ Session 6 ✦

7. According to John 10:10, what kind of life does He want us to live?

    Answer: "I [Jesus] came that they may have life, and have it abundantly [or to the full]."

8. What does "abundant life" or life lived to the full mean to you?

    Answer:

    ▲ Has a positive outlook through faith in God's love and sovereignty.

    ▲ Has a high confidence level (his confidence is really in Christ, not himself).

    ▲ Has a close relationship and open communication with God.

    ▲ Arguments with other people are resolved quickly (keeps short accounts and is a peacemaker).

    ▲ Keeps anger, anxiety, and stress under control.

    ▲ The power of God flows in and through his life.

God wants each of us to live a meaningful, significant, maximum kind of life. He understands when you become discouraged, but He also knows that you don't have to stay that way. Take the right steps to get off of the downhill, and start riding the Abundant Life Express transport that God has for you!

The Main Thing I Learned from Episode 12:

_____

_____

_____

_____

_____

Main Things:

If needed, help your son by suggesting some key truths that he should have learned during this session, such as managing discouragement, overcoming downhills, and learning to live an abundant life.

Session 7: Episodes 13 and 14 of Teknon the Champion Warriors

Episode 13: A Job to Finish

Champion Characteristics
Mental Toughness and Navigation

Power Verse: Philippians 3:13b-14

Forgetting what lies behind and reaching forward to what lies ahead, I press on toward the goal for the prize of the upward call of God in Christ Jesus.

Story Summary

As episode 13 opens, we find Teknon reeling from the disappearance of his father and Phil. He is not sure whether he should return to the safety of Northros or travel up the unknown mountain path in the hope of finding someone familiar. The only thing on Teknon's mind at this point is his own survival.

It takes an ambush by a charging amacho to jolt Teknon back into the realization that he has a larger purpose to accomplish. He defeats the creature, and determines to take up the team's original cause of retrieving the

Episode 13 Overview:

Using the choices Teknon made in this session as a launching point, you will have the opportunity to encourage your son to focus on completing worthwhile tasks as he progresses toward manhood.

If he is starting to lose his enthusiasm for completing his CHAMPION Training, remind him of your original purpose in starting it with him. Explain that one of the key traits of manhood is the ability to persevere through difficult times. Remind him, too, that he is nearly finished with his training, his celebration ceremony is close at hand, and you will soon formally recognize him as a young man.

Logos.

A pivotal event in Teknon's life takes place when he connects on a personal level with Pneuma, the Warrior King, for the first time. Teknon pledges his life to carry out Pneuma's mission. Teknon's new relationship gives him an inner peace and sense of purpose that he has not known before. Later, he triumphs over his old enemy, Rhegma, which further builds Teknon's confidence and strengthens his resolve to focus on the mission at hand. During the scuffle, Teknon discovers that he is able to utilize the features of the Hoplon that he found on the ground back by the cave. Teknon uses the shield to fly to the outskirts of Magos' fortress. He investigates a bright light and is astonished to see his father and the rest of the team waiting for him.

Discussion Topics

Choose to focus on the mission

Learn to persevere even in difficult circumstances

Connect with God and draw on His power

Reconnaissance

1. Recite the CHAMPION Warrior Creed (see page 5).

2. Review the Map of the Mission on page 8 and determine the team's location in episode 13.

3. Review the CHAMPION definition of **Mental Toughness**.

    Answer: "I will allow God to direct my thinking toward gaining common sense and wisdom. I will use discernment when making hard decisions. I will desire respect from others rather than compromise my convictions for acceptance or approval."

4. Why did Teknon decide to complete the mission on his own after he defeated the amacho?

   Answer: The incident with the amacho gave Teknon renewed confidence in his training and helped him to refocus on his purpose and his objective of completing the mission.

5. Why do you think Teknon decided to talk with Pneuma?

   Answer: He realized that he could not complete the mission in his own strength. This pushed him to recognize his own inability to save himself and his need for a dependence on Pneuma. He finally understood some of the reasons a relationship with Pneuma was so important.

Strategy and Tactics

Remembering the Lion and the Bear

The Bible tells the true story about a young man who completed his mission under very difficult conditions. His name was David. His mission: defeat a 9 foot tall giant named Goliath.

Read 1 Samuel 17:1-54

1. Describe Goliath (verses 4-11 and 43-44).

   Answer: Goliath was a champion for the Philistine people and stood over nine feet tall. He was heavily armed and vicious in speech and action.

Nobody who ever gave his best regretted it.

George Halas

Remembering the Lion …

Your son has probably heard the story of David and Goliath since he was a toddler, but encourage him to look at it from a fresh perspective. Ask him to read the story from the perspective of staying focused on your mission.

> *Success seems to be largely a matter of hanging on after others have let go.*
>
> Will Feather

2. How did David view Goliath (verse 26 and 46)?

   Answer: David viewed Goliath with loathing and disdain because the giant chose to defy the armies of the living God. David did not appear intimidated.

3. Why did David believe that he could defeat Goliath (verses 34-37 and 47)?

   Answer: David knew that he was well-trained and prepared. But, more importantly, he was aware of God's past faithfulness in his life. God had already given him strength to kill a lion and a bear. David knew that the same God who had given him victory over the lion and the bear would also give him victory over this Philistine.

4. Why did David refuse to wear King Saul's armor (verses 38-40)?

   Answer: David was not used to wearing armor; it was clumsy and slowed him down. Besides, he knew that he would not need the armor to defeat his opponent. David was convinced that God would deliver Goliath into his hands.

5. What did David use to defeat Goliath (verses 40 and 47-50)?

   Answer: David defeated Goliath by using a method and tools common to him as a shepherd. With a common sling, he hurled a stone, which was delivered under God's power directly into Goliath's forehead. The Bible calls attention to the fact that there was no sword in his hand. David didn't have a weapon, but he had something much more powerful—the almighty and living Lord of Hosts.

David was willing to face Goliath because he — a shepherd boy — remembered how God had delivered him from the lion and the bear in the fields of Israel. David knew that God was watching over him and protecting him.

How to Focus

Let's use David's example to discover some practical steps to focus so that you can accomplish important missions in your life.

- ▲ **Target your objective.** David targeted Goliath as the adversary he had to defeat for God and his country.

- ▲ **Train yourself for the mission.** David trained himself both physically and spiritually during his time as a shepherd.

- ▲ **Think of the resources** you will need to complete the mission. David carefully chose his method and the tools he needed to ensure Goliath's defeat.

- ▲ **Trust that God will use and empower you** to complete any mission that He has given you. David acknowledged at an early age that his strength came from the Lord.

- ▲ **Thank God** for His faithful commitment to provide for you so that you can complete the mission. It is very important to remember how God has been faithful to you in the past. David expressed his gratitude to God for delivering him from the lion and the bear and then from Goliath.

- ▲ **Take action to complete your mission.** David acted upon his trust in God by stepping onto the battlefield. Once he made the first step to confront Goliath, there was no turning back. The Bible says that David

The greatest honor we can give Almighty God is to live gladly because of the knowledge of His love.

Julian of Norwich

actually charged toward Goliath on the battlefield.

It's easy to become distracted from doing the important things in our lives. Sometimes even good things can prevent us from doing the best things—those things that will make the greatest long-term impact. For example, too many basketball games or too much time with friends might prevent us from spending time reading the Bible or finishing our homework.

To become a CHAMPION, you must learn to prioritize your objectives wisely. Then you must focus your mind, your time, and your resources to complete the most important objectives before moving on to the other ones. It won't be easy. But when you look at David you can see the benefits of learning how to focus.

6. What if you don't want to complete an important objective? How do you get it done if you just don't feel like it?

Sometimes you need to have the "want to" when it comes to completing a worthy objective. Sometimes, however, God directs you to achieve an important objective that is not fun or pleasant. If maturity can be identified by your ability to focus, then you show your level of maturity by your willingness to trust God, even through a task that offers little enjoyment throughout the process of completion.

7. Which important objectives do you have that you find easy to accomplish?

8. Which important objectives are tough and demand all the focus you can muster in order to get them done?

```
┌─────────────────────────────────────────────┐
│                                             │
│      THE MAIN THING I LEARNED FROM          │
│                 EPISODE 13:                 │
│      _____    │
│                                             │
│                                             │
│      _____    │
│                                             │
│                                             │
│      _____    │
│                                             │
│                                             │
│      _____    │
│                                             │
└─────────────────────────────────────────────┘
```

MAIN THINGS:

If needed, help your son by suggesting some key truths that he should have learned during this session, such as how to focus on his objectives, using the practical steps we see from David's life and how to prioritize those objectives.

Episode 14 Overview:

This session will give you an opportunity to discuss how our unique God-given bents contribute to the power of the team. We each have strengths and weaknesses. Yet God gave each of us different bents, or temperaments, so that we can all contribute in unique ways to accomplish His mission in the world. During this session, help your son to understand that he is a valuable part of God's team—and your team. Both you and he need to accept that God has given him strengths and weaknesses for a reason, and that we all need to function together in unity to be most effective.

Episode 14: Back to Back

CHAMPION Characteristics

Integrity and Attitude

Power Verse: Psalm 139:14

I give thanks to You [Lord], for I am fearfully and wonderfully made; wonderful are Your works, and my soul knows it very well.

Story Summary

In this final battle between Magos and the CHAMPION Warriors, Teknon finally participates as a vital member of the team. Teknon now personally owns the mission and realizes that Pneuma is his ultimate source of strength and protection. Teknon finds out that the Hoplon he used in episode 13 is actually a duplicate designed for him by Kratos. After receiving Kratos' final briefing, the team heads for Sheol, the enemy fortress. Magos throws everything he has at them: energy fields, footsoldiers, kakos, land mines, deadly energy beams, hidden panels, poisonous gas, doubt, deception, and scorn. Teknon has an opportunity to demonstrate what he has learned—about fighting, about himself, and about Pneuma. The team uses their individual skills and technology to overcome challenge after challenge. Teknon defeats Scandalon and then faces Dolios, who takes the form of his worst fear. Magos nearly defeats Kratos, but the team prevails.

Teknon retrieves the Logos as the team narrowly escapes Sheol before the fortress self-destructs.

Discussion Topics

Embrace the strengths and weaknesses of other people

Understand my own unique bent and value to God's team

Harness the power of a diverse team to complete a mission

Reconnaissance

It will be important for you to apply all of your "Main Thing" action points after your CHAMPION Training is complete. Over the next few years, you will have the opportunity to develop powerful habits that will advance your development toward courageous manhood. Don't stop the process! Remember what you have learned and continue the process of growth.

Recite your power verse (Philippians 3:13b-14) from episode 13.

Is there an important objective or task that you need to complete? Look again at David's example and the six T's from episode 13. Which of these will help you to focus so you can accomplish your objective? Circle them.

- ▲ Target your objective
- ▲ Train yourself for the mission
- ▲ Think of the resources you will need
- ▲ Trust that God will use and empower you
- ▲ Thank God
- ▲ Take action

Recite the CHAMPION Warrior Creed (see page 5).

1. Review the Map of the Mission on page 8 and determine the team's location in episode 14. They have finally achieved their objective of retrieving the Logos and defeating Magos! But success required tremendous team effort, a great deal of character, and dependence on Pneuma.

2. Review the CHAMPION definitions of **Integrity** and **Attitude**.

    Answer for Integrity: "I will seek to acquire a clear understanding of who I am in Christ so that I may have a deeper comprehension of what I believe, what I stand for, and how I can live out those convictions in the most difficult circumstances, whether I am alone or with others. I will allow other people to hold me accountable to standards of excellence."

    Answer for Attitude: "I will cultivate a disposition of humility. I will assume a correct and hopeful view of myself as a member of God's family. I will improve my ability to manage anger and discouragement. I will develop and enjoy an appropriate sense of humor."

3. Why do you think Kratos waited so long to let Teknon use his Hoplon?

    Answer: Teknon was not ready to receive it earlier in the mission. He needed to mature in important areas of his life before Kratos could entrust it to him.

    Tor explained to Teknon what it means to own the mission: "You gained the head knowledge about becoming a CHAMPION, but not the conviction of heart. For that, you had to face the possibility that no one else would retrieve the Logos unless you stepped in. When you did, the mission not only belonged to us, but to you as well."

4. Do you believe God has a mission for you to own? What do you think that mission might be?

5. Dolios transformed himself into Teknon's greatest fear in order to defeat him. What was Teknon's greatest fear?

   Answer: Teknon's greatest fear was to see his father as evil—a man with no convictions or purpose.

6. How did Teknon defeat Dolios?

   Answer: He sought strength from Pneuma to overcome his fear. When Teknon's fear went away, so did Dolios' power over him.

   Logos is the Greek term that means "the word." Teknon, his father, and the CHAMPION Warriors risked their lives to retrieve the Logos because of its importance to the people of Basileia. Logos is used in the Bible to refer to thoughts and expressions of God Himself delivered in spoken or written form to us. Jesus is also called the Logos because He is the ultimate expression of God's message to man.

7. Why is God's Word, the Bible, so important to us?

   Answer: Hebrew 4:12 says that God's Word is "living and active." It is not an ancient book, but rather the living and powerful messages of life given to us directly from the heart of God. The Bible shows us who God is, clarifies His mission, high-lights our value to Him, and gives us guidance for our daily lives.

Different is Dynamic:

Help your son to understand that he is indeed a valuable part of God's team and your team. Your son needs you to tell him that he is uniquely created and blessed with strengths from Almighty God to accomplish His mission here on earth. He needs to know that you love him whether the two of you are very similar or very different.

Coming together is a beginning; keeping together is progress; working together is success.

Henry Ford

✦ Session 7 ✦

8. Tor said, "There is great power in a team." What do you think he meant by that?

   Answer: Help your son to see that God has created each one of us with different strengths and weaknesses, just like each of the CHAMPION Warriors. If we work together as a team, we can compliment each other as we all seek to do His will and accomplish the mission He gives to us.

9. Kratos instructed the warriors to "watch each other's backs." Why is it important for us to watch out for each other?

   Answer: The spiritual battle we are in is just as real and just as dangerous as any physical battle. We need every member of the team to stand strong. That's why teamwork and accountability are so important. True friends encourage each other to stay on track in our attitude and behavior. We must hold each other to a high standard, care for one another, and pray for each other's success.

Let us not give up meeting together, as some are in the habit of doing, but let us encourage one another – and all the more as you see the Day approaching.

Hebrews 10:25 (NIV)

STRATEGY AND TACTICS

Different is Dynamic

It's no secret that we all have different "bents." You may like to be the point person, positioning yourself in front of the group as the leader. Or maybe you like to be in the background keeping track of details and helping get things done. Maybe you're a natural salesman: motivating, promoting, and trying to present yourself well in the process.

Does it bother you that you're not the life of the party? Do you wish that you could make friends easier? Does it bother you that you're a cautious person or don't feel comfortable leading?

The point is this: it takes different types of players to make a great team. God uniquely designed each one of us with different strengths and weaknesses. And it's a good thing that everybody isn't alike. What would the world be like if everybody was a CEO ... or an engineer ... or a salesperson ... or a farmer ... or a public speaker?! In God's plan, different is dynamic. Your unique differences provide a dynamic contribution to the mission God has for His team here on earth. To accomplish an important mission, it takes people with different bents and strengths that can fill in each other's gaps and accomplish more as a synchronized unit than any one person could accomplish alone. Be yourself and bring your unique strengths to your family, your church, or whatever team you are a part of — and make it more dynamic!

In order to have a winner, the team must have a feeling of unity; every player must put the team first — ahead of personal glory.

Paul "Bear" Bryant

How Are You Bent?

1. What do you like best about yourself? What do other people seem to like about you?

   Have you ever considered how unique and important your personal traits are in accomplishing God's plan here on earth? Did you know that God designed you specifically with His perfect plan in mind?

Quote Tip:

Ask your son, "Why is this true? How could our family work better as a team?"

2. How well does God know you? (Read Psalm 139: 1-12.) What does He know about you?

   Answer: God knows everything about you and me. He is intimately acquainted with all of our ways. He knew about us from the beginning of our existence in the womb and even before the foundation of the earth was made.

3. According to Psalm 139, who created you?

   Answer: God created each of us with a specific purpose and intent.

✦ Session 7 ✦

Main Things:

If needed, help your son by suggesting some key truths that he should have learned during this session, such as why a team needs people with different strengths or what he learned about his own bent or dealing with other types of people.

4. Describe what Psalm 139: 14-18 reveals about your design and uniqueness in God's eyes.

   Answer: (1) He is fearfully and wonderfully made, (2) He is skillfully designed, (3) He is designed for God's special purpose determined ahead of time, and (4) God put precious thought into his specific design because He cares for him.

Do you think God makes mistakes? Of course not! And according to Psalm 139, God made you just the way you are. And because He made you just the way you are, you are fear-fully and wonderfully made in His view!

The bottom line: God doesn't want a team made up of clones. God blessed you with a uniquely crafted design for His special purpose in your life. Enjoy the design He gave you and use it to be an integral part of God's team.

The Main Thing I Learned from Episode 14:

_____

_____

_____

_____

_____

Session 8: Episode 15 of Teknon and the CHAMPION Warriors

Episode 15: Celebration

CHAMPION Characteristics

Navigation and Ownership

Power Verse: 2 Timothy 4:7-8a

I have fought the good fight, I have finished the course, I have kept the faith; in the future there is laid up for me the crown of righteousness.

Story Summary

The battle is won. It's time to celebrate! Friends, family, and dignitaries join the victorious team in the flying mansion of Kratos and his wife, Paideia. The team is honored for its heroic efforts against the evil forces that threatened Basileia. Kratos publicly recognizes Teknon as a young man and a valued member of the team. Kratos took Teknon's shield from him but now returns it to his son to use for Pneuma's glory (and not his own). Admiral Ago officially revives the ancient CHAMPION fighting unit by proclaiming them the New League of CHAMPION Warriors. As the excitement of their celebration winds down, Kratos gets word of the next evil uprising detected on Basileia that requires the team's immediate attention. It seems Magos is

Session 15 Overview:

Completion of the CHAMPION Training begins a new era for you with your son. You have helped him to establish a base set of skills and a level of rapport with you that can now continue. Be his coach and cheerleader during the coming years. Help him to navigate his future course by encouraging him to set high standards in every area of his life and to trust God in all things on a daily basis. Remind him to focus on serving God and other people. Continue to provide opportunities of growth and challenge for him.

back; and there is even a bigger foe to fight. The mission continues.

Discussion Topics

Chart your course and accept your mission

Earn your "wings" so you fly on your own

Celebrate victories and give glory to God

Reconnaissance

1. Recite the CHAMPION Warrior Creed (see page 5).

2. Look again at the Map of the Mission, pause at each location in Teknon's quest, and remember what he learned. Then, review the key things you have learned on your quest for truth. Highlight three important lessons you have learned.

    Answer: (1) overcoming fear of the unknown (2) enemy assessment; embracing the mission; effective stewardship (3) sexual purity (4) discernment; choosing friends; consequences (5) teachability (6) showing honor and respect (7) avoiding sexual temptation (8) overcoming fear; recovering (9) breaking out of your comfort zone (10) resisting mediocrity (11) living your convictions; avoiding romantic entanglement (12) managing discouragement (13) choosing to focus on the mission (14) harnessing the power of the team (15) charting your course and celebrating victories

3. Review the CHAMPION definition of **Ownership**.

   Answer: "I will apply effective stewardship by using my life and the resources God entrusts to me—including my possessions, time, and talents—for His glory. I will seek contentment in God's provision for my needs. I will learn to practice delayed gratification."

4. Why do you think Kratos took Teknon's shield back from him?

   Answer: To illustrate to Teknon that he was only a steward of the shield, not the owner. Notice that it was renamed the Shield of Pneuma, identifying its true owner.

5. Why do you think Kratos returned Teknon's shield to him during the celebration?

   Answer: To communicate that Teknon should use the shield in Pneuma's service, as a faithful steward to the owner.

Kratos is a Greek word that means "power and strength." Teknon means "child" or "youth." During the CHAMPION Training, you have seen how much you should draw from your dad's strength of character and example. Take note that if you also strive to know God and draw on His power, as Teknon did with Pneuma, you will move from childhood toward becoming a young man of character and courage.

6. What did Kratos say to the group about Teknon during the ceremony?

   Answer: Kratos publicly declared that Teknon had played a vital role in the success of the team's mission, that he had grown in maturity, that he was now a key member of the New League of CHAMPION Warriors, and that he had transitioned from boyhood into young manhood.

Important Note:

It is extremely important that you continue committing the time and effort to coach your son through his teen and early adult years. It is also important that you continue to set a good example for him. Let your son know about your intention to stay involved in his life and that you look forward to growing with him in your own relationship with Christ. Remember that your children are the arrows that God has placed into your hands to shoot into the next generation. What do you want your legacy to be?

7. Why do you think it was important for the team to celebrate after its victory on Kairos?

    Answer: It is important to celebrate our God-given victories and the victories of others. While honoring other people is important, the key element of any victory celebration should be giving thanks and praise to God for His provision and faithfulness in our lives.

8. Why do you think it was important for Kratos to acknowledge Teknon as a young man to his friends and family?

    Answer: Young manhood is a significant transition that should be prepared for, recognized, and celebrated.

9. What is the team's continuing mission?

    Answer: To continue spreading the principles and teachings of the CHAMPION Warriors to the people of Basileia, and to protect them from the sinister strategies of their enemies—Magos and his master, Poneros.

> *Throughout the centuries, there were men who took the first steps down new roads armed with nothing but their own vision.*
>
> Ayn Rand

STRATEGY AND TACTICS

EARN YOUR WINGS

One of the most significant traditions in our country's history is the awarding of a military pilot's "wings." When a pilot has completed his rigorous training, he is invited to a ceremony and presented with a symbol of the rank, skill, and responsibility that he has earned. When he receives his wings, he is authorized to fly missions in the service of his country.

But just because he is awarded his wings, a pilot does not stop training. He knows that he must spend his career logging flight time, learning, training, and growing in his knowledge and piloting skills. He wants to become the best pilot that he can be.

Now that you have completed your CHAMPION Training, it's time for you to receive your "wings" and begin the flight into young manhood.

Accept the Challenge

Life was different in the mid-1800s. More than a hundred years ago, Native Americans roamed the plains and mountains of the United States. In those days, teenagers became men almost overnight. Young Indian men knew that when they reached a certain age, they were expected to provide and care for a family. They were also expected to join the rest of the warriors from their tribe in battle.

At what age would you be ready to assume responsibility for a family or be willing to fight an enemy to protect your homeland? If you were a Native American during the mid–1800s, you would have been about 14 years old.

But life is quite different for many young adults today. Instead of using their talents and resources to set worthy goals and accomplish great tasks when they're young, they usually settle for trying to get homework done in time to check Facebook. They expect too little of themselves.

You may not be in this camp, especially after finishing your CHAMPION Training. There are young

> *Bring me men to match my mountains. Bring me men to match my plans. Men with empires in their purpose, and new eras in their brains.*
>
> Sam Walter Foss

> *What kind of man would live where there is no daring? I don't believe in taking foolish chances, but nothing can be accomplished without taking any chances at all.*
>
> Charles Lindbergh

◆ Session 8 ◆

adults who make a difference in their families and communities. They remember that God is the ultimate source of their talents and resources. They are thankful for what they have and want to be good stewards. They take responsibility—helping their parents, working hard at school, reaching out to other people, learning what friendship is all about, setting the right boundaries, and so on. These young adults have learned to set high standards for themselves and they are meeting important objectives in life. They seek to know God better and to share Him with others. But remember, there's always room for growth.

10. Review the CHAMPION definition of Navigation.

Answer: "I will allow God to chart my course by accepting my mission from Him, and I will complete that mission by trusting in Him. I will study the Bible, God's Word, so I can know Him better and gain His strength and direction for my life. I will become goal-oriented by learning to focus my attention on completing worthwhile short-term and long-term objectives."

And looking at them Jesus said to them, "With people this is impossible, but with God all things are possible."

Matthew 19:26

Have you grasped through your training that God has a mission for each of us? Do you realize that He has given you the talents and resources you need to accomplish the mission He has for you? When you use your talents for God, and depend on His power, you are exercising good stewardship. You are becoming God's instrument on earth to accomplish His mission.

So what are you waiting for? Get involved in God's mission as a CHAMPION. Trust Him to accomplish the impossible in and through you, but make sure that you're doing your best to take responsibility to do all that you can to seek God and pursue excellence in every part of your life. Shouldn't you use the abilities and assets that God has given you to accomplish His goals? God's mission will unfold for you day by day if you will commit to follow Him. It's a great adventure!

One more thing ... it's time to celebrate! You've just completed the CHAMPION Training adventure. You've read the episodes, answered the questions, and discussed many topics with your dad. Take time to enjoy this victory and any other victories that you've experienced during your CHAMPION Training. God wants to celebrate the wins in your life and He wants you to celebrate with Him. Thank God for what he has done and for what He will do in and through you as you live your life as a CHAMPION.

Main Things:

If needed, help your son by suggesting some key truths that he should have learned during this session, such as how God can use him as a part of His mission here on earth, why he must focus on continuing to grow, and why it is important to celebrate our wins.

The Main Thing I Learned from Episode 15:

_____

_____

_____

_____

_____

♦ Session 8 ♦

Celebration Ceremony

If your dad is planning a celebration ceremony for you, write down the specifics here.

Dad, celebrate your son's accomplishment in completing his CHAMPION Training with a ceremony! Refer to chapter 4 of your Mentor Guide for practical tips on putting together an effective ceremony for your son.

My Celebration Ceremony will be:

Date: _____

Time: _____

Place: _____

Congratulations on a job well done!

Nike® says it, and we buy into it. You look at the "swoosh," as Nike calls it, and the phrase comes to your mind. You hear it in commercials, you see it on the billboards, and it's plastered on millions of shirts, shoes, and shorts. Over a period of time, we come to believe it only because some well-paid marketing wizards found a creative way to sell more products. Now, why don't we say that phrase all together? Ready, one, two, three:

Just Do It!

If only all of life were as easy as this slogan makes it sound. The truth is, life is a lot harder than selling trendy clothing. In fact, we can't "just do it" on our own when it comes to living a life in which we're unconditionally loved, eternally protected, and fully satisfied.

We need power to do that—a lot of power. Power that can only come from an all-powerful God who wants us to relate to Him on a personal level. Only those people who know Him and seek Him have access to God's unlimited power. He offers it as a free gift that we receive through faith in His Son, Jesus Christ.

God created us to have an abundant life now and for eternity. But He did not create us like androids that would automatically love and follow Him. He gave us a will and freedom to choose our eternal destination. What will you choose?

Are you 100% sure that, when you die, you are going to heaven? Why do you say that?

Mark on the following scale how sure you are that you have a personal relationship with God, through Jesus Christ:

Not at all sure   1   2   3   4   5   Very sure

How do you know?

_____

_____

Would you like to be 100% fully sure that you have a personal relationship with God that will guarantee your passport to heaven?

_____

_____

God's power is experienced by knowing God personally and by growing in our relationship with Him. God has provided the power necessary to fulfill His purposes and to carry out His mission for our lives. God is so eager to establish a personal, loving relationship with you that He has already made all the arrangements. He is patiently and lovingly waiting for you to respond to His invitation.

The major barrier that prevents us from knowing God personally is ignorance of who God is and what he has done for us. The following four principles will help you discover how to know God personally and experience the abundant life He promised.

 GOD LOVES YOU AND CREATED YOU TO KNOW HIM PERSONALLY.

a. **God loves you.**

"For God so loved the world, that He gave His only begotten Son, that whoever believes in Him should not perish but have eternal life." John 3:16

b. **God wants you to know Him.**

"Now this is eternal life: that they may know You, the only true God, and Jesus Christ, whom You have sent."   John 17:3 (NIV)

What prevents us from knowing God personally?

2. WE ARE SINFUL AND SEPARATED FROM GOD, SO WE CANNOT KNOW HIM PERSONALLY OR EXPERIENCE HIS LOVE AND POWER.

(Author's Note: The word sin confuses a lot of people. The word sin comes from a Greek term that was used in archery. When archers shot at the target, the distance by which their arrow missed the bull's-eye was called sin. That distance represented the degree to which the archer missed the mark of perfection. When we miss God's mark of perfection, it's called sin too. And because of sin, there is a wall that separates us from a perfectly holy God. Through the years, people have tried many things to break through that wall. Money, power, and fame are just a few of the things people have tried. None of them have worked. We all fall short of God's perfection.)

a. **Man is sinful.**

"For all have sinned and fall short of the glory of God."   Romans 3:23

b. **Man is separated.**

"For the wages of sin is death [spiritual separation from God]." Romans 6:23a

How can the canyon between God and man be bridged?

APPENDIX A: JUST DO IT!

 **Jesus Christ is the only provision for man's sin. Through Him alone we can know God personally and experience God's love.**

a. **God became a man through the Person of Jesus Christ.**

   "But the angel said to them, 'Do not be afraid; for behold, I bring you good news of great joy which will be for all the people; for today in the city of David there has been born for you a Savior, who is Christ the Lord.'"   Luke 2:10-11

b. **He died in our place.**

   "But God demonstrates His own love toward us in that while we were yet sinners, Christ died for us."   Romans 5:8

c. **He rose from the dead.**

   "Christ died for our sins according to the Scriptures … He was buried … He was raised on the third day according to the Scriptures … He appeared to Peter, then to the twelve. After that He appeared to more than five hundred."   1 Corinthians 15:3b-6a

d. **He is the only way to God.**

   "Jesus said to him, 'I am the way, and the truth, and the life; no one comes to the Father but through Me.'"   John 14:6

It is not enough to know these truths …

 **WE MUST INDIVIDUALLY RECEIVE JESUS CHRIST AS SAVIOR AND LORD; THEN WE CAN KNOW GOD PERSONALLY AND EXPERIENCE HIS LOVE.**

a. **We must receive Christ.**

"But as many as received Him, to them He gave the right to become children of God, even to those who believe in His name."   John 1:12

b. **We must receive Christ through faith.**

"For by grace you have been saved through faith; and that not of yourselves, it is the gift of God; not as a result of works, so that no one may boast."   Ephesians 2:8-9

c. **When we receive Christ we experience a new birth (read John 3:1-8).**

d. **We must receive Christ by personal invitation.**

"I am the door; if anyone enters through Me, he will be saved …" John 10:9

Receiving Christ involves turning to God from self (repentance) and trusting Christ to come into our lives to forgive us of our sins and to make us what He wants us to be. Just to agree intellectually that Jesus Christ is the Son of God and that He died on the cross for our sins is not enough. Nor is it enough to have an emotional experience. We receive Jesus Christ by faith, as an act of our will.

These two circles represent two kinds of lives:

Which circle best represents your life?

Which circle would you like to have represent your life?

You Can Receive Christ Right Now By Faith Through Prayer

God knows your heart and is not so concerned with your words as He is with the attitude of your heart. Here is a suggested life-changing prayer:

> Lord Jesus, I want to know You personally. Thank you for dying on the cross for my sins. I open the door of my life and receive You as my Savior and Lord. Thank you for forgiving me of my sins and giving me eternal life. Take control of the throne of my life. Make me the kind of person You want me to be.

If you sincerely prayed this prayer, you can know with 100% certainty that Christ is in your life and He is there to stay (Hebrews 13:5). So, you don't have to "just do it". God has already done it for you. You may or may not feel like it now, but this is the most important day of your life. To remember this major event in your life when you joined God's family, sign and date this page.

_____   _____
Signature   *Date*

What Are the Results of Placing Your Faith in Jesus Christ?

The Bible says:

1. Jesus Christ came into your life (Colossians 1:27).
2. Your sins were forgiven (Colossians 1:14).
3. You became a child of God (John 1:12)
4. You received eternal life (John 5:24).
5. You have the power to pursue intimacy with God (Romans 5:5).
6. You began the great adventure, the mission, for which God created you (John 10:10, 2 Corinthians 5:17, and 1 Thessalonians 5:18).

Mentor Guide (father's handbook)

Fiction novel

Mission Guide (son's handbook)

CHAMPION Training Adventure Program

For other Teknon and the Champion Warriors resources check out our website at www.ChampionTraining.com for:

▲ Character illustrations and descriptions

▲ Downloadable CHAMPION Creed and Code

▲ Which character are you? personality quiz

▲ New ideas for CHAMPION Training

▲ The Teknon Blog

Acknowledgments

I want to thank my wife, Ellen, for helping me to raise our children. I want to acknowledge my children, Katie, Kimberly, Kyle, and especially Casey for giving me encouragement and inspiration during the creative development of the CHAMPION Training adventure program. Thanks, kids!

About the Author

Brent Sapp lives in Orlando, Florida. When his oldest son, Casey, was nearing the teen years, Brent developed a strong desire to intentionally prepare Casey for manhood. This desire produced many creative mentoring approaches and several key character principles. Brent has adapted these key CHAMPION principles into a futuristic adventure novel for boys. He has also developed an interactive character-building program for fathers to use with their sons as a companion resource to the novel.

Brent and his wife, Ellen, have four children: Casey, Katie, Kimberly, and Kyle.

linkedin.com/in/brentsapp
facebook.com/brentsapp

About the Illustrator

Sergio Cariello is the talented free-lance illustrator behind the characters of Teknon and the CHAMPION Warriors. He also draws such well-known icons as Superman and Batman for DC Comics. In addition, he has taught at the prestigious Joe Kubert School of Cartooning and Animation. Sergio lives in Tampa, FL, with his wife, Luzia.

Recommended Resources for Your Journey

Resources for Spiritual Growth

Wild at Heart by John Eldredge (Thomas Nelson)
Tender Warrior by Stu Weber (Multnomah Books)
Desiring God by John Piper (Multnomah Books)

Resources to Make You a Better Father

Love Does by Bob Goff (Thomas Nelson)
Guardians of Purity by Julie Hiramine (Charisma House)
Raising Boys by Design by Gregory Jantz and Michael Gurian (WaterBrook Press)
Preparing Your Son for Every Man's Battle by Stephen Arterburn and Fred Stoeker (WaterBrook Press)
King Me by Steve Farrar (Moody Publishers)
Project Blessing by Kay and Julie Hiramine (Generations of Virtue)

Resources for Your Son to Read

Unbroken by Laura Hillenbrand (Random House)
Never Give In by Stephen Mansfield (Cumberland House Publishing)
Passport 2 Purity by Dennis and Barbara Rainey (father-son study, FamilyLife Publishing)
Hero: Becoming the Man She Desires by Fred Stoeker and Jasen Stoeker (WaterBrook Press)
How to Ruin Your Life by 30 by Steve Farrar (Moody Publishers)
The Ultimate Guys' Body Book by Dr. Walt Larrimore (Zondervan)

Movies

The Incredibles (2004)
The Chronicles of Narnia: The Lion, the Witch, and the Wardrobe (2005)
Cinderella Man (2005)
Ben Hur (with Charlton Heston, 1959)
The Man from Snowy River (1982)
Captain America (2011)
The Last Samurai (2003)
Swiss Family Robinson (1960)
Hondo (with John Wayne, 1953)
My Darling Clementine (with Henry Fonda, 1946)
How to Train Your Dragon 1 & 2 (2010, 2014)

CPSIA information can be obtained
at www.ICGtesting.com
Printed in the USA
LVHW060021080323
741158LV00023B/171